Before I Wake

A Spiritual Journey Into a Dream

Before I Wake

A Spiritual Journey Into a Dream

Dorothea E. Richardson

Dorothea E. Richardson
Chattanooga, TN. 37411
dororichardson@att.net

Richardson, Dorothea E
Before I Wake A Spiritual Journey Into A Dream
Dorothea E. Richardson
ISBN: 978-1-941749-45-6
Printed in the United States
4-P Publishing
Chattanooga, TN 37411

This book is dedicated to God,

Who makes all things possible!

Acknowledgements

This book never would have happened if it were not for the love and encouragement given to me by my sister's Annette and Carlotta, and my mother, Leola.

I would also like to thank Prof. Lori Miller, Laura Brown and Jessica Williams for their invaluable assistance in helping me to pull this book together.

Behold I come quickly!

Jesus Christ

CHAPTER ONE

I will speak to him in dreams.

Numbers 12:6 (NIV)

8:18 a.m. Saturday, June 15, 20_

Asingular silence surrounded me as I sat outside on the front steps of my grandmother's house hugging my knees to my slight frame. The quietness enshrouded me like the bedclothes of a mummy, and I rocked back and forth hoping that somehow the rhythmic motion would soothe my ragged nerves.

A palpable stillness that I had never known or felt before seemed to prowl on the sultry air. It stole over my skin like the prickly legs of a spider that slowly and stealthily crept towards prey caught in its web. It was an otherworldly silence that caused my breath to stop in my breast; an unearthly silence that summoned unnatural feelings of apprehension.

Breathe. I kept repeating the word to myself as if it was some mystical invocation that would thwart the uneasy foreboding that plagued my mind. Just breathe, I persisted and exhaled a long, slow, deep, breath. But, this disquieting anxiety that I felt had seized me and suspended any innate ability I possessed to think rationally. I felt as if I was on the verge of imploding from the unspent adrenaline that had assailed my mind and body.

I hugged my knees tighter as if to try and keep my nerves from completely unraveling and lashing out from my body. I continued to rock, to suppress the pervasive dread that had sunk into the pit of my stomach. I stifled a yawn with the back of my hand, desperately trying to ward off the lack of sleep that had begun to take effect. I hadn't slept for over 24 hours. I hadn't wanted to sleep. The night had been long and arduous, and I had wept inconsolably during most of those unrelenting hours. Now I sat desperately searching my mind for an unfathomable answer to the inexplicable question that I had been asking myself over and over again.

What on earth had really happened?

I closed my eyes and exhaled another deep breath. Tears started to flow again. I had no answer to that one disturbing and persistent question that seemed to plague my mind with fruitless ramblings. I placed my hands over my face as tears flowed down my cheeks. As I sniffed and wiped them away, I wondered if the newly formed grief that I felt had found a permanent place in my heart. A heart that ached to know just what had happened to my family. The inexorable memory of the incident that had occurred with my sister the previous afternoon raced through my mind like a bolt of lightning. It prompted a small shudder to stir inwardly and caused the hairs on my arms to rise. No matter how I tried, I could not shake the haunting imagery. Did I actually witness what had happened to Winn, or had I just imagined it all? Is this what Winn had been trying to tell me all along or was I caught in some hellish dream, from which I would never wake up? Even now, as my jumbled mind grappled with a fragment of the reality that lay right in front of me, I knew that this was no dream. I was very much awake.

I shook my head trying to collect my erratic thoughts. My head ached a little, and a dense mist engulfed my mind. It felt as though I was trying to fight through a great fog that had settled over me. At the moment, it was impossible to gather my thoughts. All I had were questions that seemed to defy any rational explanation about what had really happened. My thoughts deviated as images of my sister charged forward in my head. Hazy visions of the account that she had given before the disaster occurred briefly touched my memory. What if Winn was right? I quickly brushed the thought aside. If I accepted the explanation that Winn had offered ... my thoughts trailed again.

"Then that would make me as foolish as the rest of them," I quietly muttered to myself. "That would also mean that Winn was right, but now she's g-gone," my voice broke into a quiet sob. "I-I saw her ... and then I didn't." My thought process faltered again, and the tears started once more.

But, what other explanation could there be when a portion of the aftermath of yesterday's events was right in front of me? Was there some other solution for this insanity that my distressed mind would not allow me to see at the moment? Again, I had more questions than I did answers.

I closed my eyes again as tears eased down my cheeks. I was very tired, but it wasn't just from a lack of sleep. The weariness that I felt reached beyond my physical body. There had always been a restlessness deep within me. Now, it had heightened. It had begun to crash upon me like the fierce waves of an agitated sea. I had no idea where my family was, and I had no idea where to begin to look for them. If the explanation Winn offered was true, then there would be no place on earth to find them anyway.

"Souline?" A quiet, familiar, voice startled me out of my reverie.

"Gray," I whispered breathlessly, my voice still rather shaky from the spent tears. He kissed my forehead, pulled me close to him, and hugged me tightly. I rested my head against his chest and took refuge in his quiet strength. He sat down and motioned for me to sit on the step below his. He gently squeezed my shoulders and then rested his chin on top of my head. I needed someone to lean on, and I was glad that it was Grayson.

He, like Winn, had always been there for me; always kind and understanding, even when I didn't think I needed anyone. At this moment, I needed this strong man. He turned me around to face him. I smiled softly as his lean, brown hands wiped away my tears and soothed my weary spirit. I was tired and anxious about what lay ahead of me in this ever increasing madness. I tried to let my mind go blank while I rested on Gray's chest, but my thoughts kept moving back to my sister and Grandmother.

"Did you see anyone on the other streets?" I asked, trying to force my mind in another direction.

"Well," there was a slight uneasiness that tinged his voice. "I-it's like this everywhere," he hesitated a little as he waved at the unconsumed remains of the demolished twin-engine plane I had been staring at all morning. "There are houses and buildings still smoldering. Debris is scattered all over the place. I saw a few people that I didn't really know just walking around aimlessly."

I eased from his embrace and saw the anxious regard in his eyes that reflected the chaos he had taken in when he had walked around the neighborhood. His stare was eerie, as he focused on some unknown point and seemed to conjure the images he had just seen. He gave himself a mental shake in a futile attempt to clear his head.

"I also saw old man Jackson wandering around on the back street," he continued and gave a brief nod toward my next door neighbor's house. "He was calling his wife's name and carrying what looked like one of her dresses in his hands. I tried to get him to come with me, but it was like he didn't even recognize me. It was like he was in a daze. He kept asking me if I had seen Ida. The poor, old guy was in shock, I suppose."

As I listened, the tears started to flow again in earnest. I had spent most of the morning trying to get control of my emotions, trying to make sense of the insanity we had entered into, but now that Gray was here with me, I couldn't. It just didn't matter anymore. My heart ached for my family. I wanted to know where my sister and grandmother were.

"Where are they, Gray? Where did Winn and Gran go?" I lamented, voicing the one question that had been uppermost in my mind.

"Baby, I don't know," He said frankly, and gently patted my hand and allowed it to rest in his.

"You don't think I'm crazy do you? You do believe what I told you, don't you? I mean about what happened to Winn while I was talking to her yesterday?"

He stared down at me, as I looked at him with eyes that implored him to believe the story that I had relayed to him earlier concerning my sister and Grandmother. He kissed my forehead again as if weighing his words before he spoke.

"To be honest, honey, I don't know what to believe. But, after all that's happened since yesterday, I could believe just about anything." I sighed as Grayson gazed into my eyes; eyes that were now puffy and sorrow-burdened. These eyes had spent the better part of the night weeping and staring at the hardwood floor of my grandmother's living room as I paced trying to make sense of the events that had taken place yesterday afternoon. He caressed my head and allowed his fingers to brush the length of my ponytail, as a way of trying to console the grief that he saw in my eyes. "My God, what exactly has happened?" He asked this time. His spoken words echoed the thoughts that had continued to plague my mind since this extraordinary phenomenon had taken place.

There was just too much for me to try to absorb at this moment. I slowly scanned the cluster of homes that lined the street of my neighborhood. Pert little houses painted in warm whites, spring yellows, and barley beiges with contrasting shutters. Bright splashes of flowers graced each window box. They all seemed to echo the whispers of a spirit of wistfulness from a timeless era long past. Soft, sparse, white clouds rested in a clear blue sky, and well-manicured lawns smelling of freshly cut grass mocked the destruction displayed before me. I viewed the wrecked remains of the airplane that had crashed and was now settled in front of my home, and ruminating on the absurdity of its presence.

It was a perfectly beautiful day. The emerald leaves of the huge oaks that were scattered about the neighborhood danced in the warm, southern breeze. The sunlight twinkled through the summer foliage. It seemed to beckon onlookers to come and play. Any other day, Grayson and I might have spent the morning on the front porch enjoying a cup of coffee, reading the newspaper, or strolling through the neighborhood talking to old friends who might have been clipping their hedges, or watering their lawns. However, it somehow seemed a cruel irony for an airplane to have crashed and skidded several feet down the street in the middle of this serene neighborhood, before coming to rest in front of my grandmother's house. The empty shell of the plane lay in the middle of the street like a huge discarded corpse waiting to be removed for burial. The smell of the burned remains filled the air with a sickening acrid odor that floated through the atmosphere for miles. It mingled with the smells of other buildings and homes that had burned throughout the night. I had been staring at the plane for most of the morning when a sudden impulse came over me. I stood up and started walking toward the wreckage.

"Soul?" Grayson queried as if to ask with some uneasiness. "Where are you going?"

"I've got to see," I said.

"Souline," he gave an urgent call. "Honey, wait! What are you doing?" He jumped up and hurried after me. "It's been a long night, and I know you're tired ..." his voice trailed. Several times he had urged me to take a short nap, but I had refused. He now cast a dubious glance my way, as if my lack of sleep was prompting, what I'm sure he thought, my erratic behavior.

I moved as if fettered by some unseen line that pulled me toward the blackened, hollowed, shell. I reached the cockpit and stood for a moment and stared at the door. It was scratched and scorched from where the plane had struck other objects. It had plunged headlong out the sky. First striking the tops of the trees, and then bursting into flames as it hit the ground and skidded down Thrushwood Drive hurling metal and glass, snapping trees, and uprooting shrubbery. The fiery mass slid and skidded the length of two blocks, only to stop directly in front of our home with flames roaring several feet in the air.

The 9-1-1 call that Grayson made to Summerville's fire

department was one among many that did not receive an immediate response. He discovered later that many of the city's emergency rescue services had been overwhelmed with an influx of calls from every point in the city that evening. Everyone had been reporting that countless numbers of houses, buildings and vehicles, throughout the city, were in flames. Throughout the country, a host of planes had literally fallen from the sky, for reasons still to be determined. That same night, emergency services were overwhelmed by a torrential wave of calls placed by horrified Summerville residents stating that many of their loved ones had gone missing as well. Grayson had also been among those who had tried to call to report Souline's missing family members, and as of yet, still had not received a response.

"Souline, don't," he cautioned, looking as if he feared for my safety when I placed a hand on the handle of the scorched door. Ignoring his warning, I yanked on the closed door. It would not budge initially, but I gave it one good wrench with both hands, and the door pulled free.

"It's still warm," I said softly, mildly surprised by the fact. I stared into the gaping, black, cavity that seemed to taunt my grieving spirit, as the contemptuous crevice seemed to beckon me into its cruel surroundings. Everything was charred and blackened. The seats were indistinguishable, crusty and disintegrated. Sections of the instrument panel had been smashed or broken, and some parts that were plastic had melted with its metallic parts seared. The windows of the plane were cracked and singed. I heaved my body up into the offensive cockpit and desperately searched the malevolent structure. The inner hull had been greatly devoured by the flames, and some parts had twisted after it struck the ground. There was very little left that was recognizable except the crumbled shell itself, and that horrible scorched smell that I hated.

"Nothing!" I spat out vehemently. My voice reflected the disappointment that I felt. I heaved a great sigh. "I've been asking myself over and over again what had happened. I supposed I was hoping to find some answer in this mess. I don't know why I felt that I would find an answer here in all of this." I waved my hands about, indicating the plane. "I just want to know where they've all gone."

Grayson watched with distress as my eyes began to brim with tears again. I wiped a careless hand across my face and turned to leave the plane. He jumped down and helped me down from the cockpit, and I brushed my hands together to remove the soot that had gathered on them, closed the door, and turned to walk away. I started to move and hesitated for a split second. Just as I was about to walk away, a vague emotion fluttered within me.

"What had I seen?" I asked aloud, my brows snapped together. I suddenly turned on my heels, grabbed the handle of the door and yanked it open again.

"Souline, what's wrong?" Grayson asked puzzled when I began to scrutinize the plane once again. "What are you looking for?"

"I saw something ..." I said, trying to recapture the elusive image, as I allowed my eyes to roam over the demolished cockpit. I frantically examined the plane wreckage as if I was gathering and deciphering information at a crime scene.

"Something like what?" he asked, wondering what had prompted my re-inspection of the downed craft.

"Gray, what do you see?" I asked, shaking his arm with a sudden hint of enthusiasm.

He looked at me and said, "Sweetheart, I think that you should try and get some sleep. You've been up all night and..."

"Don't patronize me, Grayson Garrett!" I snapped cutting him off. "Look inside and tell me what you see," I demanded, my excitement rising.

Nearing the point of exasperation, he threw up his hands and sighed. "I see a burnt out cockpit." I cut him a withering glance that would have made any other man cringe inside, but he patiently took a deep breath and said, "Okay, I don't see anything! Everything is burned to a crisp."

"Look!" I pointed toward the floor of the cockpit where my eyes had finally rested near the pilot's seat.

He looked at me, frustration carved on his usually very placid face and said with an impatient sigh, "Souline, I ..."

I cut him off once again, "That looks like part of a shoe!"

He blinked, and looked slightly nonplussed when he saw where I pointed. I climbed into the mangled metal once more, stooped, and tugged at the burnt, rubbery, substance that had stuck to the floor of the cockpit. He hopped in beside me and pulled at the charred substance until it finally gave way. It was the sole of a man's work boot with the heel and most of the leather upper still attached. Grayson jumped down from the plane, and I followed. I looked at him and began to pace, as my mind started to grapple with the implications of the find.

"Gray, where are the remains of the pilot? I mean, there should be some evidence of a body, don't you think?" This is part of what my mind had been wrestling with for most of the morning. When the plane crashed, because of the lack of response from the fire department, some of the neighbors used their garden hoses to extinguish the flames. After the amateur firefighters had spent a few hours battling the flames, their communal efforts began to pay off, and they were able to contain the blaze. Once they had extinguished the fire, they searched what was left of the cockpit, but were puzzled that there was no sign of a pilot.

"Even after an intense blaze, there would be some charred evidence of a body." I reiterated. The safety glass kept most of the splintered front windows intact," I pointed out. "And the side windows are too small for an adult to climb through." I stared at him almost daring him to disagree with me.

"Well, honey, the pilot could have jumped out before it crashed," he offered reasonably.

"Okay," I allowed. "But, why would he jump out of a plane without his shoes?" His brows furrowed slightly, and after reflecting, he had to admit that it was a little strange for someone to leave their shoes behind.

He shrugged, "Maybe he had an extra pair that was near the cockpit, and they got tossed around. I don't know."

"Fine," I snapped with indignation. "But, what about the other vehicles throughout the city? Everyone keeps saying that cars and trucks have been abandoned as well. Did everyone just all of a sudden start jumping out of their cars too? Had everyone gone completely insane and purposefully ran automobiles into perfectly normal houses or propelled planes into buildings or down perfectly normal neighborhood streets? Huh, will you answer me that?" My voice started to rise and sound a bit shrill. My gestures reflected my frustration.

He gave a slight nod to indicate that he acknowledged the reasoning behind the point that I made, but I knew that he was trying to keep me from becoming upset again. I had been agitated all morning and he knew that my lack of sleep and the absence family was beginning to wear on my nerves.

"Sweetheart, calm down," he soothed and reached for me. I snatched my arm from him and started to walk away from the plane carrying the charred shoe.

"I don't want to calm down!" I shrieked and shook the sooty shoe at him. "I want answers!" I demanded, tears springing to my eyes. "I want to know what's going on! I want to know where everybody's gone! I want to know where my family is!" I started sobbing uncontrollably, and he moved from the plane and reached for me once again. This time, I allowed him to hug me. "They're gone, Gray," I wailed. "They're all gone. You won't believe what I told you, but I know what I saw."

He picked me up and cradled me in his arms as if I was a small child that needed comforting. He carried me back across the street. I held on to the burnt shoe as if it was going to unlock some great mystery about the events that had taken place. He was about to take me into the house when for some irrational reason, a wave of panic seized me, and I became agitated and almost jumped from his arms. I felt an overpowering sense of fear and I could not go back into that house.

"No," I pushed at his chest. "I don't want to go back in there! She's gone! They're gone, and I don't want to see where they left! No!" I was struggling in earnest and came dangerously close to causing us both to take a tumble. He quickly placed me on my feet.

"Okay, okay!" he said, quickly and soothingly, and began to gently caress my back, to help me to calm down.

We sat back down on the porch steps and he began to rock me slowly. The fierce tide of emotion and tears that had overtaken me started to recede and my distress slowly subsided. He suggested that we go back to his apartment, and we both took comfort in the fact that I would not be left alone at the house.

Grayson went into the house and left me long enough to gather a few of my belongings. He checked to make sure everything was secured while I sat on the porch steps. I heard him give a restless sigh, and I turned to look at him through the screened door. Those dark eyes seemed to say, "She is usually, so strong and confident, and now she seems so small and vulnerable." I turned away from that look, and pulled my knees toward me and began to rock again. My head was starting to ache again. We had been through a lot since yesterday I thought wryly, and I had an uneasy feeling that this was just the beginning of our unprecedented destinies.

"Listen!" I said, when he locked the door he walked onto the porch and leaned against one of the posts.

"Listen to what, baby?" He responded, and glanced down at me with slightly furrowed brows, as he wondered at what I had heard.

"Can't you hear it?" I insisted.

Grayson cocked his head to one side to listen, focusing his attention on his surroundings. "Honey, I don't hear anything."

"That's what I mean," I said. He looked slightly puzzled and regarded me with some apprehension, wondering if I had finally reached an emotional limit. "Gray," I continued, "Have you ever known it to be so quiet?"

He listened and realized that after the flurry of activity that had taken place yesterday, there was an odd, almost eerie, calm on the air. It was as if the whole world had become strangely quiet. He had felt unsettled all day and had passed it off as apprehension from the overwhelming activity of events that had occurred. But now, he realized that it was this pervasive quiet that had settled around them that seemed almost tangible; like a living thing and he found it slightly unnerving. It enveloped them like a slow, sleepy vapor, creeping on the air and seizing its victims.

It made him feel uneasy as if everything that had taken place yesterday was just a prelude to extraordinary events that he felt sure were coming.

CHAPTER TWO

Do not be wise in your own eyes.

Proverbs 3:7 (NIV)

9:56 a.m. Saturday, June 15, 20 __

Grayson watched Souline as she slept. She had insisted that she was not sleepy, but when he had gone into the kitchen to make coffee, he returned to find her curled up on the sofa asleep. He glanced at his watch and was mildly surprised to find that it was only a few minutes before ten o'clock.

"Man!" he muttered to himself. "It seemed a lifetime longer," he thought. He placed the coffee cup on the table and eased the coverlet he had taken from his bed over her and caressed her cheek with his finger. So much had happened to them in such a short period of time. It was as if the world around them had literally changed in a split second. How could things have changed so quickly and so radically in less than 24 hours? The most disturbing thing of all was that no one knew exactly what had happened.

Before I Wake

He had turned on the television when they first arrived at the apartment. Special news reports were filtering in from all over the world. There were reports of plane crashes, train derailments, and boating incidents. The reports of abandoned cars and vehicles were becoming insurmountable. There were also reports of houses and buildings on fire; accidents of every extreme. The broadcasts were coming in from every place imaginable. However, the most startling of the accounts were those of missing persons that were mounting by the thousands, hourly. These reports were of every age, race, and nationality and they were coming in from every walk of life and from every point on the globe. What does it all mean? He asked himself for the one-hundredth time. Why would people suddenly go missing? Why would they behave in such a peculiar manner? Why would they take such radical measures to abandon homes, jobs, spouses, children, and belongings? What was the reasoning behind all of this and where had they all gone? He wondered if maybe it was a conspiracy of some kind, but who would take on such an extraordinary endeavor, and to what end? What would be their motive, and why take some people and leave others? What would those who were taken have in common? Then again, what are the similarities of those who were left on earth?

He shrugged his shoulders, unable to solve the puzzle that plagued his mind. He sipped his coffee and paced the room.

Earlier, while he and Souline were driving his motorcycle on their way to his apartment, they both noticed that there were small heaps of clothing and belongings that dotted the sidewalks, streets, and even in some of the vacated automobiles. It was almost as if the people that were in them had just disapp...

"No," he firmly admonished himself and shook his head as he allowed the thought to trail. I am not going to do this. It's bad enough that Souline had been rambling on about this nonsense. I'm certainly not going to entertain those absurd notions, he reflected. "They will put both of us in padded cells right next to each other if I start to give into this foolishness. And now, I'm standing here talking to myself," he chided. "They'll be coming for us for sure," he said, as a wry smile touched his lips and he gave a brief chuckle.

However, the more he allowed himself to examine the circumstances surrounding yesterday's event, the less it seemed like foolishness. What exactly *had* caused this extraordinary phenomenon to occur? Grayson's brows creased as he thought about the possibilities and began to pace the length of the living room floor of his apartment again.

The room was smart with a sparse, minimalist appearance. There were a couple of neo-deco chairs, a stylish coffee table, an entertainment and music system, and a sleek, comfortable sofa on which Souline now shifted as she slept. He had inherited a built-in bookcase that spanned the length of one side of the room, which he had filled immediately after moving into the apartment. Truth be told, the bookcase was the main selling point for him when he purchased the apartment. Grayson was addicted to literature. He would read anything he could get into his hands. There were often stacks of books by his bed in various stages of assimilation; they were either being read, about to be read, or had been read.

Before I Wake

His bedroom was off to his right, down a narrow corridor where large windows with blinds faced the street below. There was a full bathroom, a large bed, a dresser, and two small reading tables. Both reading tables were overrun by massive stacks of books. At the front of the apartment, there was a moderate kitchen area. Two sliding glass doors led to a terrace where he enjoyed sitting in the evening. The terrace faced west, and he often watched the sun's descent from the evening sky.

His brows snapped together as he took another sip of coffee. He continued to pace the floor. It has been said, he thought, that there have been cases where human beings have actually experienced spontaneous combustion, but, not all at once. He stopped in the middle of the floor and absently stroked his chin. That would mean that there would have been some cataclysmic event for something like that to occur with so many people. You would also have to question the sporadic occurrences worldwide. Which means, you would have to ask again, why it happened to some people and not all? Then, you would still have to explain the clothing. Wouldn't they have ignited as well? Wouldn't there have been some physical evidence of the fire and some human remains? For a split second his mind flashed back to the charred but empty cockpit of the airplane. There was nobody left on the plane, he remembered. He shook his head to clear his mind.

What am I thinking? He chided himself once again, sighed in exasperation and moved toward the kitchen. It would be easier to believe Souline, he thought with a hint of cynicism.

He picked up the coffee pot from its resting place on the

counter, poured another cup and placed the pot back in the receptacle. He strolled toward the only window in the room and leaned against the refrigerator to peer outside.

From his third story window, he could still see piles of clothing scattered on the streets and walkways below. Surprisingly, the clothing had not yet been scooped up or taken by looters. Maybe they were afraid that what had happened to the previous owners might happen to them.

Something else puzzled him. Why would people just leave clothing, grocery bags, cell phones, jewelry, and some other personal articles on the streets? There were even women's handbags, although by now, many had been routed through by thieves and tossed aside. But still, what woman would leave her purse behind?

Now, what he knew about women would barely fill a thimble, Grayson smiled as he thought to himself. However, he understood enough to know that no woman would ever go off and leave her purse unattended, no matter what she did with her clothing. It was as if each one of those convenient, compartmentalized, carryalls, possessed some mystery that most men were not invited to know.

Even other women were not allowed to peer into another woman's purse. So, Grayson found himself wondering what would cause an inordinate number of women, to leave one of their most valued and personal possessions unattended on the streets? What would prompt such bizarre behavior? Could Souline be right about the disappearance of her sister? Was there some supernatural force at work here? Was there something more than he was allowing himself to see?

Before I Wake

The answer escaped him and he stroked his chin again as he contemplated the thought.

He ran water into the empty coffee cup that he had sat in the sink and walked back into the living room to check on Souline.

He allowed a sigh to escape his lips as he smiled down at her. Her dark, velvety lashes caressed her smooth, brown, cheeks as she slept. Her skin was the color of sweet caramel and she was beautiful. He had always thought so and unconsciously sighed again. Even when little boys were not supposed to think such things about little girls. He had known her since grade school. Even then, she was warm, caring and smart, with deep, intelligent eyes. She had a way of making you feel as though you were a lifelong friend the moment you met her. She could make you feel at ease without seeming superficial. She was slender, fit, and graceful. She wore her raven black hair at shoulders length and often changed her style to fit her moods. He shoved his hands in his pant pockets and thought with amusement of Souline's many moods.

He and Souline had always been kindred spirits and were as close as two people could be who were unrelated. They had both lost their parents when they were very young and had both been raised by their grandparents. They attended the same elementary, middle, and high schools and had basically grown up in the same neighborhood. He had lived on Fairmont Lane, which was two streets over from Thrushwood Drive where Mrs. Mary Thrasher, Souline's grandmother, lived. His grandfather had died of heart disease and her grandfather had died of lung cancer. He moved out of his grandmother's house when he started his first year at community college. During his second year at college, his grandmother passed and Souline and her family became his adopted family. When they were growing up, he and Souline ate together, played together, argued, made-up, and sometimes as friends often do, they consoled each other when the world seemed to push a little too hard. They had always been there for each other, and he knew that as long as he lived, he would always be there when she needed him.

There were times when he thought that he could feel her heartbeat even though she was miles away. No matter what she did, or where in the world she would go, he knew that he would always be a part of her life.

Souline shifted once more on the sofa and murmured something unintelligible as she did and settled back into a gentle slumber. He smiled at her and pulled the coverlet back over her from where she had kicked it to the floor. Her breathing was deep and steady and he hoped that she would sleep for at least a few more hours because she needed the rest. To say that yesterday's experiences had been overwhelming for her would have been an understatement. His mind went back to the call he had received from her yesterday.

5:04 p.m.: June 14, 20__

Grayson worked for Winter Gates Realtors, and he had an afternoon appointment to show a house to a couple in the Misty Mountain Subdivision on the east side of town. The newly developed subdivision was fairly exclusive, and many of Summerville's young up and coming professionals were flocking to the area because of the rising economic development in the area. For them, it was a way of making an imposing, but non-threatening statement in the southern community. It was their way of saying that they were educated, savvy, and well-to-do. In short, they had arrived.

Grayson had just walked out of the office when his cell phone rang. He could hear the extremely agitated voice on the other end desperately crying and trying to explain about her family.

"Gray?" She sounded wild and excited.

"Souline?" he queried and frowned wondering why she sounded so hysterical.

"W-Winn, Winn's gone! I saw her, but she's not there. I-I was holding her hand!" Souline stammered.

"Souline?" He called, but she cut him off.

"They, she-she's gone and I can't find Gran either!" She wailed.

"Souline, baby calm down! Listen..." he tried to interpose but knew that she was not listening. "Honey, please try and listen..." He desperately tried again but realized that she had lost all sense of equanimity. "I'm supposed to show this couple a house, but I'll reschedule and be over in about fifteen minutes. Okay? Do you hear me? Souline, just calm down!"

He was yelling over the phone in a desperate attempt to get her attention. She was crying uncontrollably and he knew that she was distracted.

"Gray, Winn is gone and I need to find Gran!" She said.

"Souline!" he yelled. "Soul..."

The phone went dead.

Grayson felt himself go rigid.

In all of the years he had known her, Grayson could not recall a single moment when she had ever behaved in such a disturbing way. He hurried to find her.

Grayson usually drove the sedan when he had to show homes, but when the Tate's had said that they would meet him at the subdivision he had driven his motorcycle to work instead. He tried to phone David Tate to change the appointment, but he could not get through. Grayson left a voice message instead, stating that a family emergency had arisen, and he would reschedule the appointment early next week, and that he was sorry for the inconvenience. At the time, he had no idea that he would never show the house to the couple because he would later learn that the Tate's would also be counted among those listed as missing.

When Grayson got on the road heading toward downtown, the cacophony of horns blaring in the distance, had not registered in his mind at that moment as being part of the event occurring worldwide; the event that had caused Summerville traffic to become so snarled. In truth, why would such a notion ever occur to him?

Assuming there had been an accident, he turned off the main road to take the less traveled back streets of Summerville. He had wanted to avoid the throng of vehicles that were beginning to gather into what would eventually become a cohesive mass of vehicles entwined with some of their human hosts.

The collective chaos would last for several weeks.

Before I Wake

It was warm, and sunlight winked through the dark foliage that filled the tree-lined streets. Large clusters of blood red, crape myrtle hung low on their branches offering startling splashes of color along the otherwise somber vista. Houses closely aligned with their neighbors were tucked away in shadowed recesses that were hidden by tall hedges or fences that shielded their inhabitants from on-lookers navigating along the road.

Grayson could feel the sun riding on his back as he continued on his trek toward Thrushwood Drive. White lines that marked the road were a blur beneath his wheels as he devoured miles of gray-black asphalt, speeding towards his destination. He wondered what could have possibly happened to cause Souline to reach such a level of hysteria. Growing up together, he had seen her, agitated, exasperated, and downright infuriated, but he had never known her to be completely out of control.

He had been so preoccupied with his thoughts that he did not immediately notice the two cars that were oddly parked on the side of the street. However, he did notice a pick-up truck that had stopped horizontally in the middle of the road, after having to swerve to avoid running into it. He also saw that the driver was nowhere to be found. Frustrated, he offered, under his breath, an unflattering commentary about today's hapless drivers and the overall rudeness of modern society. He was about to speed past the truck when he saw an overturned car that had landed on its passenger's side in a shallow ditch. He realized this may have been the reason the truck driver stopped. He circled back around in the road toward the car, to see if anyone had been injured or if they might need assistance. He parked the bike, got off, and jumped down into the shallow ditch to peer into the car, only to discover that there was no one in the vehicle and the motor was still running. Grayson hopped up on the car to try to open the doors, but they were locked. He peered through the windows to make sure that there was no one in the back seat and saw no signs of life. The only things he did see in the front seat were a few articles of women's clothing, shoes, a cell phone and a handbag that had slid over to the passenger's side against the window. In the back seat, a teddy bear, an infant's carry-all and baby clothing tangled in an infant car seat.

"That's odd," he said.

He was just about to get on his bike when his curiosity got the best of him. A strong impulse seized him to take a look into the pick-up truck. He looked in and saw that there was a pair of jeans, a plaid shirt slumped on the seat and a pair of work boots on the floor of the cab.

"Okay, that's just too weird," He said to himself, as he hopped back onto his bike and headed back down the road. He wondered if he might come upon the drivers of both vehicles somewhere along the road to offer some assistance if he could. Maybe they got out safely, he reflected. Maybe the guy in the truck got out to help. Then the thought suddenly struck him that there could possibly be a man, a woman and her infant walking along this back road completely undressed. As he considered the notion, the corners of his mouth turned up into a faint smile. Surely not! But, why were their clothes still in their cars? There were a few more cars he had passed that had been askew on the narrow road, so much so, that he had to bob and weave his way through portions of the street as he drove. Why would the drivers of the automobiles park so haphazardly, he wondered? Just as Grayson was maneuvering down a small summit of the street, there had been a slight incline in the road. He approached someone who was driving at a snail's pace heading down the incline. He stayed behind the car for a moment and then decided to move around to pass the car. As he went around, he turned to look at the driver, and as he did, he blinked and did a double take.

"What the devil?" he exclaimed in disbelief when he drove past the car. He saw that the automobile was moving but had no driver. He stopped long enough to watch in amazement, as the car inched its way toward the left, crossed the road, and with a relatively light *tap*, the car stopped next to a telephone pole with its rear end protruding onto the street. Once again allowing his curiosity to govern him, he drove around and peered into the automobile only to see two heaps of clothing, one set belonging to a man, the other to a woman, deposited on the front seat as if they had been rapidly deprived of their owners.

"What in the world is going on?" he mumbled incredulously, through his helmet. He looked around to see if anyone else had seen the bizarre spectacle he had just witnessed on the road; but, there was not a soul in sight. He circled the bike around, turned back onto the road, and sped toward the Thrasher home. The odd incidents had made him a little edgy. He wanted to get to Souline as quickly as possible.

It was not until later that evening, however, when it occurred to him that he never did find the occupants of either of the vehicles. He wondered if they might also be counted among the missing. Grayson had just turned onto Ridgecrest Terrace, which was about three blocks away from Souline's when he saw a group of people standing outside of a house. A black SUV had inadvertently run head-long into the living room of one of the homes.

"Has everybody gone crazy?" He exclaimed to himself, with mounting apprehension, shaking his head in amazement and darting away. He had lived most of his life in this neighborhood. In many ways, it had escaped the insanity of the world at large. It was a closely knit community, usually very tranquil and had the good fortune of housing neighbors that still cared about others. He saw that several of the residents had gathered on their lawns talking in small clusters; some angry, some frantic and gesturing wildly, and some even crying hysterically. He wondered if some collective madness had seized the community. His mind immediately raced back to Souline and the behavior she had exhibited when she was on the phone with him. His insides instinctively tightened. He hurried to find her.

By the time Grayson reached her, she was an emotional wreck. She was with her next door neighbor, Moses Jackson, standing on the front lawn of her home. Grayson could see that Mr. Jackson was desperately trying to calm her.

Mr. Jackson had come home from work and noticed that his wife, Ida, was not in the house. He knew that she often lost track of time when she was gossiping with Souline's grandmother, Mary. He was on his way to see if Ida was visiting with her next door neighbor when Souline had all but assailed the old gentleman as she tried to explain what had happened to her sister. She had been on her way to his house to see if her grandmother had visited his wife.

Grayson had driven the bike up on the lawn next to the house, hopped off and hurried toward the two, tossing his helmet on the seat. Souline's arms were waving wildly as she tried to explain her dilemma to Mr. Jackson. She was trying to coax the older man into following her and was frantically pulling him by the arm toward her house. She was still crying and looking quite shaken when Grayson ran to her. She looked lost and confused as if she did not really recognize him.

"Souline," he spoke firmly. When she did not immediately respond to him, he realized that she was in shock. Grayson took her by the shoulders and gently shook her to try to bring her back to herself.

"She...they," she gulped and sniffed. There was a distant look of desperation in her eyes that tugged at Grayson's heart. He had never seen her so shaken.

"Souline, look at me. Calm down," he said. He ran a gentle hand up and down her back trying to ease her agitation.

"B-but, sh-she's gone!" Her cry was guttural and harsh. It came in fitful spasms that racked her graceful frame as she spoke in small catches. "I-I saw her, b-but she's not there. I mean she-she's gone! They're gone!" Her face was contorted and wet with tears. Her face was etched with great pain and anguish.

He knew that he needed to calm her down. "Souline, Souline,

look at me!" Again, Grayson spoke firmly and shook her gently once more. Her soulful brown eyes seemed to return from the faraway place they had been.

"Gray? They're gone!" She lamented. "Where have you been? Winn and Gran... they're gone!" She looked at him as if she finally recognized him, and she grabbed him and hugged him with all of her strength.

"Shh-shhh," he said, soothingly as he hugged her. He placed his chin on top of her head and began to rock her from side to side, still trying to ease the fierce emotional upheaval that had taken hold of her. He continued to rub her back as he rocked her and he could feel her relaxing a little.

Mr. Jackson gave a shy smile toward the young couple, shifting his weight from one side then to the other, feeling like an interloper as they embraced. He pushed one hand into the pocket of his overalls and took the old cap off he was wearing to scratch his head.

"Everythin's gonna be all right, chil'" He said rather uncomfortably in a baritone voice edged with a strong southern dialect that rumbled when he spoke. His eyes shifted furtively from one then to the other. "I was jus' lookin' for my Ida when..."

Mr. Jackson never finished his explanation, because just at that moment Grayson's head popped up from Souline's like a jack-in-the-box.

"What is that?" his eyes narrowed and he pointed to the object in question. The elderly man turned and Souline peeped out from Grayson's embrace when she felt his body tense. She and Mr. Jackson allowed their eyes to follow to where his finger directed. Grayson, still perplexed, continued to stare until his face suddenly registered astonishment when the full realization of what was coming toward them settled in his shocked and amazed eyes.

The next few moments for Grayson took on a slightly surreal quality. He literally hoisted Souline around the waist and grabbed Mr. Jackson by the arm and with every bit of strength he possessed he pulled them both and ran toward the side of the Thrasher's home.

In the distance, Grayson saw a huge mass streak across the blue sky toward them. The sun glinted on the white and blue structure that was hurling out of the warm, summer sky. A plume of blue-grey smoke snaked like a huge python coiled around the tail of the plane, as the plane sped uncontrollably toward the earth.

Grayson remembered feeling as if everything had slowed down, and as if he was moving through ripples of gelatin. Souline struggled out of his grasp and nearly fell over the grill that was stored near the house. Mr. Jackson was thrust backward against a honeysuckle bush that grew by the side of the Thrasher house. When they were at a safe distance, the trio turned and watched the horrific scene unfurl with a dreadful fascination.

The massive structure lopped off the top of some of the neighboring trees, as it descended. One of the wings struck a tree, and the branch was flung with great force into one of the neighbor's front windows. Sparks flew from the underbelly of the plane. As it hit the ground and skidded down the street, the plane burst into flames. The other wing of the plane seemed to twist like paper, as it smashed into an automobile that was parked on the street and continued to barrel down the block. Someone driving a red pick-up truck desperately made a sharp turn off into one of the neighboring yards, to avoid striking the moving mass. Some of the residents of the community either ran to move out of harm's way or poked their heads out of doors to see what was causing the calamity.

The flaming malformation began to lose its momentum, as it skidded down Thrushwood. Just as the plane came to rest in front of the Thrasher's home, there was an extraordinary explosion that caused the ground to shake. A huge fireball escaped upward from beneath the aircraft. Smoke from the plane billowed for blocks. Several of the neighbors ran to see the spectacle, but the heat was too intense to get near the craft.

Grayson was one among several people to call emergency services about the incident, only to be told that there were several other accidents that had occurred throughout the city. They promised they would be there as soon as it was humanly possible.

CHAPTER THREE

For we are but of yesterday and know nothing, because our days are but a shadow.

Job 8:9 (KJV)

1:28 p.m. Saturday, June 15, 20___

Disjointed imagery filled my mind like colorful shards of glass spinning and floating in open space. Each shiny fragment displayed snapshots of a dream imprinted on my soul. I stirred on the sofa and abruptly awoke from a restless sleep, finding my tattered emotions as disturbing as the broken images that streamed through my mind. I bolted upright from my sleep, panting and perspiring as if I had been running. My sleepy mind searched the room and collected what initially seemed to be unfamiliar surroundings until full recognition that I was in Grayson's apartment and not my own bedroom registered in my mind. The mid-day sun had splashed into the room and left delicate patches of light on the walls and floor as the warm, hazy, sunlight filtered into the room. I squinted a little and then my eyes focused on Grayson, who sat asleep in one of the chairs across the room with his legs outstretched. He held the remote control in his relaxed hand. He had turned the volume on the television up just enough to be able to catch what was being said as various news reports streamed across the screen.

The room was relatively quiet, except the subdued tones of the television and the deep release of breath that Grayson expelled while sleeping. I crossed my legs beneath me, pulled the pillow that I had been resting on underneath my chin and turned my attention toward the television to listen to the news report.

The image of a handsome, seasoned, anchorman flashed across the screen as he announced, "We go now to Andrea Burke, who is standing by in Atlanta with an unusual traffic report."

"Thank you, Steven," replied the well-dressed, polished reporter. She continued, "I'm here live in Atlanta Georgia, where at any other time it would be impossible to attempt this; but, I'm standing in the middle of I-75. As you can see behind me, *I'm on the road that leads to nowhere.*"

She stretched her arm out and turned. As she spoke the camera slowly pulled out to show the massive tangle of automobiles that had littered the interstate behind her.

"There are literally thousands of vehicles that have been wrecked or abandoned on the highway due to the unprecedented event that took place yesterday afternoon. Rescue and emergency services have been working throughout the night checking vehicles to remove the injured and the dead. From the numerous reports that we have received, the most unusual of the reports are from the survivors claiming that their loved ones have just vanished into thin air."

A close-up image of a young, Caucasian male, in his mid-twenties, flashed across the television screen.

Souline buried the lower part of her face into the pillow and pulled it tighter to her as she listened intently.

"I had jus' picked up mah wife and son," he said. "An' we was drivin' here along the highway, on our way home," he directed his thumb and nodded toward the interstate behind him. "When Angie, mah wife, and mah four-year-old son, Dusty, jus' *poof*, disappeared right in front of me. I was doin' 'bout seventy-five miles, so I know that they didn't jus' jump out of mah pickup truck. I mean, why would they? 'Sides I woulda' seen that. I jus' wanna know where mah family is. I jus' wanna know what's goin' on."

The young man's face looked drawn and haggard, and his pallor made him look well beyond his years. Tears began to weld up in his eyes. It was obvious that he had been greatly affected by the incident.

The reporter continued, "Traffic started backing up along the interstate just after the five o'clock rush hour yesterday. Many of the occupants of the vehicles were said to have had friends and family members to vanish while they were in transit. Eyewitnesses said that a number of the vehicles continued to move even after the occupants had disappeared, causing countless accidents along the I-75 corridor. Many were forced to abandon their vehicles after traffic became too congested to maneuver through. Authorities are saying that it may take several weeks to find the owners of these vehicles, or to have wrecking services to clear the roadways. What we are also finding, is that the massive traffic jams are not limited to just this stretch of highway, but similar incidents have happened on all of our nation's interstates and roadways. Similar accidents are being reported worldwide. This is Andrea Burke reporting from Atlanta Georgia. Back to you, Steven."

"Andrea has anyone given an explanation as to what may have caused these alleged vanishings?" he asked.

"No, Steven. Emergency crews are still examining many of the vehicles that were left on the highway. They have their hands full searching for those who are injured or who may have died in the crashes. They say it may be weeks, even months before they can give an accurate account of what may have actually happened. While searching some of the automobiles, our own news crew observed that many of the doors were locked, and in some cases the engines were still running. However, one of the more interesting points was that there were articles of clothing left on the seats of many of the abandoned vehicles as if their owners had either disrobed or indeed disappeared. Officials are reporting that the President is having a State of the Union address later today, and many of the world leaders are calling for an emergency summit to discuss what impact this event might have globally. Steven."

"Thank you. That was Andrea Burke reporting from Atlanta. Now, we join our overseas correspondent, Jean-Luc Dubois, who is in Paris, France to report on the U.S. and French ambassadors who are also among the missing..."

I was riveted to the television. I shivered inwardly as I watched the images flash in and out of the contained space. I felt slightly nauseous and I still had a bit of a headache.

There were people from all over the world that had been reported missing. There had also been an extraordinary number of bizarre accidents that had occurred worldwide due to this event. I thought about my sister and the conversation that we were having just before she...

It was hard for me to reconcile exactly what had happened to my family just at the moment. Whenever I tried to think, my mind would not allow me to look at the situation rationally. It was as if I had a vapid space in part of my brain and nothing made sense once it reached that point. It was like some great, mental, black hole that swallowed the light of reason and would not allow it to shine through. I stared at the television, unseeing. My mind raced back and forth over yesterday's events wondering if I had missed anything that would help me to bring some order to my chaotic thoughts.

Suddenly, an impulse seized me. Desperation clutched at my insides like a steel vise. I knew that I had to do something, anything, to try and figure out what happened to my family.

I looked over at Grayson, who had barely stirred the whole time I had been watching the news reports. His keys were on the coffee table where he had placed them earlier. Judging by his deep breathing, he would probably sleep for another hour or two, which would give me plenty of time to go home and come back.

I slowly eased my body off the sofa and out of the coverlet that entangled me. I briefly glanced at Grayson and thought that I should probably leave him a note to explain my whereabouts just in case he woke up before I got back. He might think I've disappeared as well, I thought wryly. I carefully routed through my purse for a sticky-note, scribbled a quick message on the pad and stuck the neon yellow piece of paper in the middle of the television screen. I quietly gathered his keys from the coffee table and tipped quietly across the floor, only to pause for a second when the wood gave a tiny creek as I headed out of the door.

He never moved.

I took the elevator down and went out to the apartment parking lot. The fresh air seemed to revive me and helped to clear my head a little. I hesitated for a moment trying to decide if I should take the sedan or the motorcycle. I felt the first smile settle on my face since yesterday as the memory of Grayson teaching me to ride that monstrous bike flashed through my mind.

It had been so much fun racing through the streets of our neighborhood as I learned to maneuver, *Black Beauty*, the name he had christened the bike. As I became more confident over the weeks, I would take the downtown streets or explore some of the dirt roads in our hill country that were a lot more challenging. All the while, Grayson would encourage me, telling me that I could do anything I put my mind to. I loved the freedom I felt when I drove the bike; it was a wonderful and exhilarating feeling.

But right at this moment, I didn't feel very adventurous. As a matter of fact, I felt small and alone. I felt a great shift in my universe and I wasn't sure how to set things right again. I had not rested well when I slept, and my nerves were still too raw and frayed. I didn't think that my stomach and head would take the jolts too well either. I would feel better and safer taking the car. I needed time to focus, time to think things through. If I could, I needed to go back into my grandmother's house to try to determine what exactly had happened to my family.

I slid into the sedan and immediately felt the heat from the leather seats that had been ravished by the mid-day sun. I eased out of the parking space and headed for my Grandmother's house. Instead of going through the town where I knew the road would still be congested with abandoned cars, I decided to take the back streets to get to my house.

Large trees loomed like a great, green, canopy and sporadically blocked the afternoon sunlight as I drove through the eerily silent streets. The narrow back streets were rarely overrun with traffic during the normal course of a day, but I had been driving for almost fifteen minutes and had not encountered one single living soul driving down the road.

As I drove, I noticed that some cars I passed along the road seemed as if they had been abruptly abandoned, not just merely stopped and parked by their drivers. I even saw the one car that Grayson had told me about that was still on its side in a shallow ditch. The pick-up truck, however, was no longer in the middle of the road. It had been pushed or parked to the side of the street. I wondered if the people who had driven those vehicles might have been among those who had... I shook my head to clear the thought. I desperately tried to keep my mind on the task of driving, but there was an ominous sensation closing in on me that I could not quite shake. There was a strange feeling of foreboding that would not grant me the solace of a concrete solution to the problem of my missing family members. Every time I passed one of those *oddly parked* vehicles, as Grayson called them, I had an overwhelming urge to jump out of the car, run over, and peek into one of them, hoping I could find some clue as to what had happened. But I fought the irresistible urge and kept driving toward home.

I noticed that some of the homes had also suffered similar damage like those in my neighborhood. Not only had the cars been damaged, but, I saw where the elegant, two-story home that I had always admired when I drove through this neighborhood, was now ashes and blackened timber. I turned on the radio hoping that the music would soothe my frazzled nerves. But the airways were filled with tragic stories of the dead and missing. I did not want to hear them. I snapped off the radio and drove in total silence.

I turned onto Ridgecrest Terrace and saw the bright yellow house that the SUV had crashed into. The house had been boarded up on its front left side with plywood. The black SUV, now parked on the front lawn, was totaled from where it had plunged head-long into the living area of the home. I wondered if the car accident had occurred because it had been robbed of its owner. I hoped that no one had been seriously injured.

I drove slowly and noticed that there were varying degrees of chaos that appeared throughout the neighborhood. I saw the sidewalks dotted with clothing and wondered if they belonged to friends.

I continued onto Thrushwood, only to see much of the same mayhem that I had just witnessed on the previous streets. I stared at the odious aircraft that prevented me from parking in front of my own house and finally pulled up in front of the Jackson's house. I released a long sigh and wistfully regarded my grandmother's home. It was a large, wooden-framed house painted white with dark gray shutters. It had a large, gray front porch. Two patio chairs rested on the porch and a swing hung from a dark gray, wooden ceiling. Several potted plants growing profusely out of their ceramic homes, due to my Grandmother's green thumb, lined the porch as if to beckon *welcome* to anyone visiting our home.

The house sat squarely on a full acre of land and exhibited a beautiful lawn that was the envy of many of our neighbors during our numerous family and neighborhood gatherings.

I propped my chin on my hands as they rested on the steering wheel and allowed the memories of past family gatherings to fill my mind. I remembered birthday parties, family reunions, barbecues, and neighborhood get-togethers where people were always happy. I wiped away hot tears that had stolen down my cheeks and sighed at the poignant memories. I smiled at the fact that my grandmother never needed an occasion to invite people into our home. She loved when the house was filled with cheerful, laughing people.

I got out of the car and walked toward the house. I glanced at the piece of shoe that we had pulled from the plane. I had an overwhelming desire to kick that shoe, feeling as if it had betrayed me by not offering any answers to my pervasive questions.

Before I Wake

I snubbed the scrap and walked past it wondering about the owner of the abandoned footwear. Where was he? Had he jumped out of the plane as Gray had suggested or had he gone the way of my family? I shrugged my shoulder in response to my unanswered questions.

I felt around in my purse for my door key. I found my key, stuck it into the lock, straightened my shoulders, took a deep breath, reached somewhere deep inside of me to summon all of my strength and courage before opening the front door. I squinted and allowed my eyes to adjust to the dimmer light that enveloped the living room. As my eyes became accustomed to the light, I realized that nothing had changed.

Everything was the same.

The house boasted of a rather large living room, with a connecting dining area, a full kitchen, three bedrooms, each with a bath, and a den that Gran turned into a music room for Winn. Gran had wanted both of us to have the benefit of piano lessons when we were in grade school. However, Winn excelled at piano. After Gran had observed that I had a natural inclination toward dancing, she made sure I took ballet lessons.

Being young, I never thought of the sacrifices she and Granddaddy must have made for the private lessons, but she always encouraged us and never complained about the expense. Both Winn and I attended college and became teachers. She taught music at Anderson High and also became the choral director at her church, Pleasant View Baptist. I received my BFA in education so I could teach ballet, modern and interpretive dance. I now instruct at the Summerville School of Performing and Creative Arts.

I sighed and looked around the living room. Somehow, I had expected things to have changed, but nothing had. Why should there be any change?

It was just that so much had changed around me since yesterday and I felt as if everything else should have done so as well. I walked around the house touching objects that had special meaning for me since my childhood. I ran my hand across my grandfather's mahogany pipe stand that my grandmother kept filled with his favorite pipes over the fireplace, even though he has been dead for several years. I fingered the beautiful, lead, crystal candy bowl that Winn and I had saved up for so that we could give it to Gran as a Christmas gift when we were children. It was always filled with peppermint. A fleeting smile played across my lips at those happy memories. I walked over to the music room and ran my fingers over the keys of my sister's piano. I also made a mental note to water Gran's potted plants that were peppered around the room.

No, nothing had changed.

I had been so foolish. There was no reason for me to have been afraid to come into the house. There was nothing here that could hurt me. Everything in this place was a testament of people who had loved me and those who I loved in return. I turned slowly to leave the music room to go upstairs. Granddaddy Joe had had a motorized stair lift installed for Gran, right after she had a stroke that paralyzed her from the waist down. I ran my fingers over the burgundy velvet chair of the lift as I climbed the stairs.

I stopped and observed the navy and white, cotton dress, and the blue, fuzzy, slippers Gran had worn yesterday, that still lay on the lift that had stopped in between floors. The memory was still fresh enough to cause tears to brim in my eyes. Winn's clothes were still on the floor in the kitchen, I recalled. I ran my hands up and down my arms to smooth the hairs that had risen when I gave a little inward shiver. Tears flowed down my face and I caressed my grandmother's dress as if it was a precious treasure. I touched it to my face and inhaled the sweet hint of vanilla that she always wore.

"Where are you?" I whispered on a sob.

I carefully placed the dress back on the chair, turned, and walked upstairs toward the door that led to my sister's room. I regarded the simple, but attractive, room as I lingered at the threshold for a moment; allowing my eyes to lovingly touch on the mementos and photographs of the past that were placed around the room.

It was a restful and inviting place. The walls were painted mint green with a cool white trim and there was a matching print comforter and coverlet that lay on the bed. The fireplace, when in use, chased away many harsh winter nights. It often added a peaceful glow to the room as well as to my spirit. Memories of Winn and I sitting and talking for hours on end before a cozy blaze filled my mind. The blaze from the fireplace would dance before us seemingly eavesdropping on our conversations.

On the dressing table were articles that Winn cherished. There was a picture of the two of us with our mother and father, as well as a sterling silver comb and brush set that I had given her for her sixteenth birthday. There was also a picture of Gran and Granddaddy Joe, and other little trinkets that she had collected over the years. I walked over and picked up a black and white photo of us on roller skates. We were about seven and nine-years-old, Grayson was in the middle, hugging us each around our necks with a goofy, toothy, grin. Granddaddy Joe had taken it with an old box camera, to show us how it worked.

Suddenly a surge of memories engulfed me.

I remembered when Grayson taught both of us to roller blade, and I smiled a little remembering the scar I still had from when he patched up an awful scrape that I got when I had fallen.

There was also that time when Winn and I helped granddaddy build the swing set in the backyard. I remembered when we played hop-scotch when we baked cookies with Gran, and the time we sneaked and picked green apples from Mr. Jackson's tree and got sick from eating them. With the photo still in hand, I flung myself on Winn's bed and wept bitterly.

"Why did you leave me?" I moaned. "Why does everyone always leave me?" I lay on the bed as the wretched tears overtook me and I sobbed wildly over the loss of my family. I wondered if it was just the loss of my family members that caused my heart to grieve so intensely, or was there something more. Was there some other inexplicable grief that I had been grappling with long before this all started? I did not know. All I did know was that my family was no longer with me and the deprivation was more than I could bear. I ached to know where they were. I felt so lost and so alone without them. I cried until the sobs finally subsided.

I rolled over on my side and as I did, my hand touched a book that lay behind me. I instinctively knew that it was Winn's Bible. I pulled it to me and hugged it because it made me feel closer to my sister. I ran my hand over the gold, engraved letters on the front of the book that read, The *Holy Bible*, and underneath in the right-hand corner, it said, *Winsome Thrasher*.

Just then, my mind raced back to last Sunday; the last time I'd held this book. Had it only been a week?

I remembered I had been sitting on the edge of this very bed watching Winn get dressed for church. She was rushing around in a pretty, white-laced satin slip, searching for a pair of pantyhose that did not have a run in them.

CHAPTER FOUR

Who can hide in secret places so that I cannot see them?"
declares the LORD "Do I not fill heaven and earth?"

Jer. 23:24 NIV

8:45 a.m. Sunday, June 9, 20____

"For goodness sake, Souline," the pretty, petite, figure darted around the cool, confines of her bedroom, trying to remember where she had placed the pantyhose that she had just had in her hands. "You should give the man a break. He's in love with you and don't give me that look as if you don't know what I'm talking about." I had cast an askance glance toward Winn just as she spotted her hose draped over her vanity chair across the room.

"I'm not looking at you any particular way," I objected mildly. "I just know how I feel about Gray. Sometimes he gets too serious about things concerning us and I'm just not sure if I'm ready to settle down right now, that's all. Besides it's not like he has actually asked me to marry him, you know." I said, a bit peevishly.

"Well, he will, and you're not getting any younger you know?" Winn wrinkled her nose at me and smiled.

"And twenty-four, isn't exactly ancient either," I said.

"I know, but still, Souline, you should consider his feelings." She scolded mildly.

"I do, but why doesn't anyone ever consider my feelings?"

"Aargh!" Winn gave a low, frustrated growl as she examined the pantyhose. "I can't believe that I just put a hole in my brand new pantyhose. Satan is so busy this morning. But, he is not going to keep me from going to church today. Souline, please..., please tell me that you have a pair that I can borrow."

"Maybe," I said impishly. "Or maybe I'll let you go to church bare-legged or with a big ole' hole in your hose," I said grinning at her.

"Souline...please?" she whined, biting her lower lip and placing her hands together as if to pray.

"Well, believe it or not, my dear sister," I smiled back at her. "I bought a couple of pairs just the other day. The color might be a little light, but I think you can get away with wearing them."

"I don't care if they are multi-colored. If I don't get a move on, I'm going to be late." She lamented. "I'm playing for the youth choir this morning and it's difficult to get them together sometimes," She added.

I dashed from the bed, glad for the opportunity to escape the subject of Grayson, which she tenaciously pursued at times. I ran next door to my bedroom and returned with a box of coffee-colored hose.

Upon re-entering the bedroom, I promptly stopped in the doorway of the room, when I noticed that she was motionless and her vision seemed transfixed on some unseen object.

"Winn?" I spoke softly and approached her cautiously. When I took a couple of steps into the room, she responded by giving her head a little shake. She seemed bewildered when she saw that I had come back into the room. She shifted slightly from her rigid position as if she was coming out of a trance and back to life.

My brows furrowed and I inquired, "Are you okay?" I walked over and placed a hand on her shoulder when she swayed slightly.

"Yes, yes, I-I'm fine," she stammered a little and looked slightly confused by my presence.

"Here, sit down," I said, concerned about her behavior, prompting her to move toward the chair near her dressing table.

She rebuffed the action, by gently pushing my hands away. "Will you stop clucking over me like some mother hen? I'm alright," she smiled weakly. "Really, I am. Where are those pantyhose? I'm going to be late for church."

"Let me get you some water?" I moved to go toward the bathroom.

"No, really, Souline, I'm fine." She waved a delicate little hand and gently took hold of my shoulders, to steer me toward her bed and pressed downward on my shoulders. "Sit," she demanded. "Now where are those hose?" she insisted. Winn had become her old self, bright and animated once again.

A wane smile played across my lips and I scrutinized her under my eyelashes, as she tried to manage a balancing act while putting on the pantyhose. She seemed fine. She rocked and reeled on one foot and then the other in the middle of the floor while gently pulling and tugging on the footwear. I watched the slight figure race around the room and marveled at just how much she looked like our mom. She was the same diminutive version of her.

She had inherited mom's beautiful, dark, even complexion, her full mouth, and her slightly slanted brown eyes, that seemed to lend a rather pixie-like quality to her overall appearance. Like mom, she had a kind nature that prompted her to help anyone in need. However, Winn had a very straightforward and pragmatic approach to life. When she was defending her views and beliefs, she was a lot like a bulldog with a bone. She never let go. Gran always said that those were qualities she had definitely inherited from our dad.

"Are you sure you're okay?" I asked as she stepped into her dress.

"Yes, yes! Don't be silly," she said, with some impatience, and buttoned up the front of her navy-blue dress.

I lay across the bed on my stomach and thumbed through the Bible that had been resting on her bed.

"Come go with me," she said, watching me from under her dark lashes as I perused the book.

"What, to church? No thanks." I said, shaking my head. "Why do you always ask me that?" I mused.

"I guess because I want you to come with me," she said, frankly. "We used to go with Mama when we were children. She would want you to go."

"Yeah, but she's not here, is she?" I spoke rather sharply and with a touch of bitterness, and she looked up surprised by my tone. I noticed the wounded look on her face. "I'm sorry," I said, contritely.

"She would want you to go, Souline," she insisted softly and crossed the room to pat my hand to acknowledge the apology.

"Winn, please..." I begged because I knew that she was building towards one of her lectures on the merits of going to church.

"What happened to you?" She asked, and sat on the end of the bed. She cast a sympathetic glance toward me as she carefully smoothed her hands over the silky pantyhose to make sure they were not twisted. "What made you drift away?"

My eyes rested on the cover of the Bible unseeing, absently running my index finger over the gold letters that said, Holy Bible, and shrugged my shoulders not wanting to get into a debate with her.

"That's not an answer." She prodded gently, pressing for an answer to a question that I did not wish to give. Frankly, I wasn't sure I had an answer for that probing inquiry.

"Well," I said, as I rolled off the bed and bounced to my feet. "That's the only answer that you're going to get. I've got to see if Gran needs any help." I kissed the top of her head and shot out of the door before she could ask me anything.

I let out a long breath as I moved down toward the other end of the hallway to my Grandmother's room. I did not want to get into a conversation about religion with Winn. It always started and ended the same way. I would sit and listen to her go on and on, about the virtues of being a Christian and the salvation of Christ; and afterward, I would find myself feeling frustrated, guilty, and defensive. I just did not feel like going through that routine this morning and having my stomach in knots. I tried to understand the religious philosophy of my sister and grandmother, but I could never figure out what was so great about being a Christian. What was so great about a God who took my mother away when I needed her most in my life? I love my grandmother and know that no one could love Winn or me more, but I missed my mom and there wasn't a single day that went by that I didn't think about her. I just did not want to discuss the matter. Not even with Winn.

Our mother, Joycelyn, had been an RN in the trauma unit at the County General Hospital. Our dad, Jonathan, had died in a tragic car accident when I was only two and Winn was four years- old, leaving mom alone to raise us.

Mom had possessed a naturally kind and giving nature. She was someone who would take in stray dogs and cats, and would give her last dime to anyone if it meant the difference between them eating or going hungry. I had often wondered if her love for helping others was the reason she had chosen nursing as a profession.

One evening, on her way home from work, she was shot during a convenience store robbery, leaving us then, ages six and eight for our grandparents to bring up; I never got over losing her.

I felt a pang of loneliness shoot through me, as I knocked on the open door and walked into my grandmother's bedroom. I found her sitting at her dressing table brushing her hair into a tidy chignon.

"You're not going with us again this Sunday?" she asked,

looking into the mirror and training her sharp eyes on me as I drew near and kissed her on the cheek.

"Oh, Gran, not you too?" I complained, hugging her. "I just got the same lecture from Winn."

"Well, baby, it's just that we care about you and we miss that beautiful smiling face of yours when you're not with us."

"I know, but you said that it's my decision didn't you?" I looked at our reflections in the mirror as I hugged her around the neck and rested my chin on top of her stately silver head.

"Yes, I know, and it is your decision baby. It's just that now is the time to give your life to Christ while you're still young and able to do His work."

"Gran, *please.*" I hedged and lifted my head from hers. I felt the sensation of frustration starting to build again.

"I just want what's best for you. I love you and you know that. But God loves you more. This old world we live in is getting worse by the day. It won't be long before we see its end.

"Gran..." I moaned, with a slight frown.

"Now, I know that I'm not a rich woman, and I couldn't give you the best of material things that this world had to offer; but, I tried to lead you in the ways of Christ so that you could have the best spiritual gifts that God had to offer."

"I know," I said, sighing, gently rubbing her shoulders and hoping she would soon change the subject. I lifted the lid of a small ceramic box that lay on her dressing table which held slender black hair pins.

"And I know too," she looked up over her spectacles at my reflection in the mirror, as I added hair pins to her bun to help keep it in place. "I know that there's a lot of pent up anger inside you, and you've got a lot of pain that you've been carrying around since your Mama died."

She had touched a nerve and I flinched inwardly.

"Gran, please, I really don't want to talk about it. Okay?" I looked at my Grandmother in the mirror once again. "*Please?*" I implored, trying to coax her out of the lecture that she had started.

"Alright," she lifted her hands and conceded with an easy shrug of her shoulders. "I'll let it go, but sooner or later you're going to have to let go of that anger that you're holding on to, or it's going to rob you of your salvation. I just hope that it's sooner and not later."

I averted my eyes from her piercing gaze in the mirror. It was as if she was looking beyond my face into somewhere deep inside of me that I did not want her to see. I concentrated on the task of pinning her hair.

She gave a dry chuckle. "Now button this old lady up, so that I can finish dressing for church," she said, patting me on my hand.

"Yes ma'am," I sighed. Relief washed over my tense body, and I was glad that she had not launched into one of her hour-long sermons. I kissed her on top of the regal head that I had finished pinning, and deftly buttoned the tiny pearl buttons that lined the back of the cream silk dress she wore.

When I finished, I sat in a rocking chair that was perched near the foot of Gran's bed and watched as the handsome woman navigated her electric wheelchair effortlessly around the room preparing for church. She was someone who seemed to possess a timeless beauty. My grandmother and I were closer in color than Winn and I. Her face was a caramel color that was smooth and elegant. She had a long, graceful neck, a regal nose, full lips, and piercing dark brown eyes that seemed to unearth the deepest of secrets of a person's character. She was innately honest, generous to a fault, and she possessed an indomitable spirit that never seemed to falter. Life never seemed to get her down. That's not to say that she did not have concerns, even hardships, because she did. But, she never allowed them to rule her life. She just seemed to take life's bumps and bruises in stride. Maybe that was her beauty secret; not her outward appearance but her inner strength was her true beauty.

I remember one afternoon when we were younger, Winn and I got off the school bus. Our neighbor, Mrs. Jackson met us and told us that Granddaddy Joe had taken Gran to the hospital. We were to stay with her until he returned. Granddaddy came the next morning to collect us, with the news that a stroke had caused severe nerve damage, and that Gran would be paralyzed from the waist down. I remember my grandmother's initial frustration when she struggled with trying to find new ways to cope with her everyday chores and simple tasks. But, I would often hear her say, "For Thy lovingkindness is before mine eyes, and I shall walk in truth." Little by little she overcame the frustrations and learned to manage very well.

It was difficult for a ten-year-old to comprehend why she would say such a thing when she was unable to walk. As I got older, I came to understand that the scripture was about her faith in God. As the years passed it never dwindled. I wondered why she never blamed God for taking away her ability to walk. Gran would chuckle and tell people, "Honey, now that I've got wheels, I can move faster than ever!"

"Would you hand me that box, please?" The question eased me from my daydream.

"Yes, ma'am." I walked to the head of the bed and retrieved the beautiful, blue and white, floral satin hatbox that held one of her treasured adornments.

I removed the box top and helped her place a sassy, creamy, white straw hat, donned with a wide, organza ribbon and stunning silk flowers on her head.

Gran tilted her head from side to side, as she observed her image in the mirror until she nodded with approval at her reflection.

"Am I ready, honey?" she chuckled, asking the question she had asked me every Sunday after she finished dressing.

"You're ready to knock 'em for a loop, Gran," was the reply I always gave her and kissed her cheek, every Sunday since we had started living with her.

I helped Winn put Gran into our handicap accessible van, and waved a solicitous hand as they drove off to church. I turned toward the house and breathed in the magnolia blossoms that filled the summer air like a heady intoxicant.

It was early morning and already humid. The light breeze that rustled the heavy, rich, magnolia leaves did nothing to relieve the heat. The sticky humidity hung in the air like a warm sheath that clung to the skin. I had wanted to sit out on the porch swing and read to take my mind off of the morning lectures, but I knew that if I stayed outside for ten minutes I would need to shower again.

I was about to enter the house when a familiar horn blew. I turned to see Grayson waving at me as he pulled up to the curb. I walked toward the silver sedan, and he pushed a button to lower the window facing me.

"Hey, beautiful," an engaging smile played across his handsome face.

"Hey, good looking, whatcha' know?" I responded returning the smile.

"Nothing much," he grinned.

"Why are you up so early?" I asked, still smiling as I leaned through the passenger window of the car.

"I have a house to show at noon, so I thought I'd grab some breakfast before I did. I wondered if you wanted to join me."

"Sure," I gave an impudent grin. "Let me lock up, okay?"

It took me less than five minutes to change my shoes, give myself a quick glance in the living room mirror, check the house to make sure nothing was amiss, and lock the door.

I dashed from the house, jumped into the car, and Grayson eased the automobile from the curb and glided onto the road toward town.

CHAPTER FIVE

I perceived that this also is vexation of spirit.

Ecclesiastes 1:17 (KJV)

10:22 a.m. Sunday, June 9, 20__

Grayson chanced a side glance as he pulled away from the curb and saw that Souline was lost in thought. He decided to concentrate on the task of driving to allow her the luxury of solitude as he steered them toward town. Light from the summer sun played now and again across her face while she leaned her head against the headrest and watched the houses pass into and out of her view.

They had been driving for about twenty minutes before he pulled into the parking lot of the *Gourmet Griddle*, one of the more popular eateries. However, there were very few people in the restaurant during this time of the morning, so he pulled into the lot with ease. He parked and walked around to the passenger's side to help Souline out of the car.

It was no big surprise that there were hardly any people in the restaurant. The southern town of Summerville housed hearty, viable, people who were hardworking and church going.

The town boasted of having a church on nearly every corner in many of its neighborhoods, and a great percentage of the residents practiced the ritual of attending church on most Sunday mornings. Some church services would be an all-day event if members felt it necessary. There was also a host of mid-week prayer times and other meetings during the week. However, Grayson knew that it would not be long before the church doors would be flung open, and the parishioners begin to fill many of the local businesses including the *Gourmet Griddle*.

A pretty brunette waitress, named Vickie led them to a table next to a window. She took their drink orders, handed them each a menu, and disappeared behind a pair of swinging doors that led to the kitchen.

Souline sighed and stared out of the window to watch a robin that had perched itself on a sign that read *No Parking, Loading Only*. She thought that the bird obviously had no regard for rules, smiled at her whimsy and released another tiny sigh.

"Soul, is anything wrong?" Grayson finally chanced an inquiry.

"No," she shook her head and sighed once more.

"There's that sigh again," he said. "That's the third time you've done that since we've been sitting here. Not to mention, I noticed that you did it several times while we were driving here. What's bothering you, baby?" He reached over and caressed the side of her face with his finger.

"Oh, it's nothing," she hedged and then said, "and everything." The waitress promptly returned to the table with a steaming pot of hot coffee, poured two cups, took their food orders, and retreated again behind those doors.

Grayson watched placidly as Souline's slender, deft, fingers added sugar and cream to her coffee. He sank back into the red vinyl booth to sip his dark brew without the additives. She seemed to drift into a state of contemplation as she stared absently into the cup and rhythmically stirred the creamy, rich liquid.

"So?" He broke the silence with the quiet inquiry. "Are you going to tell me what's bugging you?" He said, still curious as he watched her stir the hot beverage.

"Like I said, it's nothing." She took a sip of the coffee and felt the warm liquid tumble through her body.

"And everything." He stated, and a sympathetic smile moved gently across his lips.

She looked over the top of her cup and was warmed by the smile that he offered her, more than the liquid that she drank.

"Oh-hhh...," she drawled and seemed to weigh her thoughts before she spoke. "It's just that Winn and Gran started in on that same old church thing again," She stated, with a hint of frustration.

He rendered a noncommittal, "Oh."

As a rule, Grayson did not like to get into the religious debates that Souline and her family often had. He tried to stay neutral, simply because he was fond of each of them, and he knew that his views were so different from theirs. He did not deny that there was a God, nor did he affirm his existence. Her family was so passionate about their beliefs, and he often found their fervor fascinating. There were many times when he had wanted to discuss their religion with them but felt it prudent to forego the debate for Souline's sake.

"Oh?" she snapped. "Is that all you have to say?" Souline immediately apologized for her testy reply. "I'm sorry, Gray. It's just that sometimes they get on my nerves with all of that church talk."

He waved away the apology and asked what happened. The waitress returned, placed their food on the table, refilled their cups and moved to another table in her designated area.

"I don't understand them," she continued, with mild agitation. He looked at her as he sprinkled pepper on his scrambled eggs and thought it best just to listen. "They're always asking me, why I don't come to church with them? Or, how come I don't get more involved in church activities, or why don't I join the church? I swear, Gray, it so aggravating. Then for some reason, Gran started talking about Mama this morning. She said that I was angry and that I needed to let it go!"

Souline continued to vent for about fifteen solid minutes, and he allowed her to release her frustrations without interruption. The waitress started toward their table to ask if they needed anything, but the handsome face looked over Souline's graceful head, that was now bobbing as she gave a running account of her family's spiritual views, and gave the waitress a telling glance with a barely perceived shake of his own head. The waitress smiled her acknowledgment, gave a brief nod, and turned her attention towards another customer.

"I'm not like them, Gray," she continued. "They can sit and listen to Pastor Martin for hours, but I just can't get that worked up about all of that God stuff."

Her monologue finally slowed, and she paused for a moment before she asked with eyes that reflected uncertainty, "Does that make me a bad person?"

"No, of course not," he offered. "It just means that you have a different view than they do, that's all."

"I just don't believe in all of those bells and whistles, and I'm not going to pretend that I do just to appease them," she said emphatically.

"I don't think that they would want you to anyway, sweetheart," he said evenly. "I think that they have your best interest at heart. I'm sure that they mean well."

"I'm sure that they do," she agreed with a sigh. "It's just that I get so frustrated always having to defend my feelings."

"I know." He said, gently caressing her hand and the tension seemed to flow from her lovely face. He knew that unless she directly posed a question to him or asked for his help, it was best to allow the topic to wane. He realized that she was just letting off a little steam and that she needed time to sort things out in her way. Souline shifted the conversation when she asked about the house he was showing, and they took their time to enjoy the rest of the meal.

When they finished eating, he drove her back to the house, walked her to the door, and promised that he would talk to her later. She kissed him lightly on the cheek and retreated from the heavy humidity to seek solace inside where the cool air embraced and refreshed her at once.

CHAPTER SIX

Leave her alone. She is deeply troubled, but the Lord has not told me what it is. –
2 Kings 4:24 (NLV)

11:47 a.m. Sunday, June 9, 20__

Poor Grayson, I thought. I felt a little guilty about having spent most of the morning unleashing my pinned up frustrations on him. I admit that I could have handled my anger a little better, but he never seemed to mind when I need to talk to him about my family problems. He never complained. He just sits and listens. I've always appreciated the fact that I can go to him with any concern, and he has been willing to help me without reproach or criticism. We've always been there for each other.

Maybe Winn is right. Maybe I should start thinking about a more solid relationship with him. Quite frankly, I could do worse.
He's always been kind to me, even when we were children. We've always been best friends. Isn't that what married people should be to each other? I mean, if you can't be anything else, for goodness sake you should be friends. He's strong and dependable and certainly not mean-spirited. I can't ever remember a time that he has said an unkind

word to me, and I do care for him. I've never cared for any one man the way I do for him. But, I just don't know if I'm ready to commit to something as concrete as marriage.

I allowed a sigh to escape from my lips. I turned on the television, plopped down on the sofa, slipped off my shoes, and flipped through the channels until I finally rested on one of the twenty-four-hour news channels.

The immediate response from the screen was, "A suicide bomber killed ten people and injured at least 30 others in an open marketplace..., The next story began..., Seven children all under the age of twelve were found murdered apparently by their father..."

Although I was usually grateful to have the house to myself, this morning was proving to be a little trying. I felt anxious, and I was not quite sure why. I was accustomed to the religious rhetoric that my family doled out from time to time, but I felt as if I was wrestling with something else. Something that I could not quite identify, and for some reason I felt as though it might be connected to my mother's death.

The solitude whispered to me now, as if beckoning my thoughts to wind out of their depths and float to the surface of my conscious. Thoughts that I was not sure I was ready to face, at the moment.

My mind caught snatches of the news event an anchorwoman relayed..., "A man walked into a convenience store and opened fire killing five people...," An involuntarily sharp intake of breath escaped my lips and my heart skipped a beat.

What makes a person kill? I wondered for the millionth time as

I listened to the barrage of news reports that filled the airway. I recognized the awful hatred and the sheer evil of putting an end to someone's life; and yet every day somewhere, someone, seemed to think it necessary to commit such an atrocious act. The proof being the countless news reports that flashed across the television screen every day.

I felt hot tears swell at the back of my eyes. Why did that man kill my mother? I was always amazed that even after all of these years, this acknowledgment still had the power to unsettle me. Do the murderers forget their humanity and just stop caring? What makes a person take another person's life?

I eased my head down on the pillow and clumsily tugged at the teal blue and white crocheted blanket that had been thrown over the back of the sofa to cover myself. I fingered the delicate weave of the blanket Gran had given me when I was a child, and sleep came to me as tears spilled from my eyes.

As I slept, I wandered aimlessly, for what seemed like hours, through the images of unsolved puzzles that seemed familiar but were broken portraits of faces and places that moved in and out of my dreams. They were faces of family members that had long passed from this earth. Then I saw her...

I woke to the sound of my grandmother and sister coming in from church. The remnants of a recurring dream that often disturbed my sleep dissipated when I heard the door open.

"Mama?" I whispered, and opened my eyes to the sound of my grandmother's voice.

"I want you to go upstairs and lie down." I heard Gran say in a voice filled with concern.

"Gran, really I'm okay," Winn said trying to ease the older woman's anxiety.

"I still want you to go and put your feet up for a while," she demanded as she wheeled around to stop Winn from going into the kitchen. "And, I don't need any help cooking Sunday dinner. Thank you!"

"What's wrong?" I popped my sleepy head up from the sofa.

"Nothing, Gran's making a fuss about nothing," Winn sighed.

"I don't call fainting, nothing," Gran said defensively.

"You fainted!?" This time I jumped up from the sofa, the final fragments of sleep disappearing from my foggy brain. "You've never fainted in your life! Come and sit down." I insisted, patting the sofa and plumping the pillow that had just served as a resting place for me.

"Now don't you start," Winn said stiffly, as I literally pulled her around on the sofa and forced her to sit down.

"What happened?" I demanded.

"Nothing really," Winn said, with a light chuckle and a frivolous wave of her hand. I folded my arms across my chest and looked at her with a fierce determination that indicated that I was in no mood for arguing. "Well..." she faltered and cleared her throat nervously. "I'm not sure," she said, biting her lower lip.

Her brows snapped together as she tried to remember what she had been doing before the incident. "I was standing in front of the painting hanging in the Fellowship Hall. You know the one that has the angels ascending and descending from heaven? I think it's a depiction of Jacob's ladder."

I nodded impatiently as I barely recalled the picture.

"Well," Winn continued. "I was studying it and the next thing I remember is Gran leaning over me waving a fan and someone sticking smelling salts up my nose. I don't remember feeling dizzy or anything."

I scrutinized my sister, wondering if there might be a more serious underlying condition.

"Maybe you should go up and lie down." You think we should take her to the emergency room?" I asked Gran.

"No," came an emphatic reply from my sister, who was now on her feet. "Now that's where I draw the line." She lifted her chin stubbornly in defiance to the suggestion. Just then, there was a light tapping on the front door.

All heads turned toward the door and uttered "Come in," as a communal response.

"Hello," chimed the warm, friendly voice of our next door neighbor as she came through.

"Hello, Ida," Gran greeted the woman who was still decked out in her church attire. She was wearing a beautiful, periwinkle, shantung silk suit, with matching pumps, and a stunning periwinkle blue straw hat, with two large white roses on the side. Around her neck, she wore a short strand pearl necklace that lay perfectly on the white blouse she was sporting. A pair of delicate pearl earrings pierced her plump ears.

"How is she?" Mrs. Jackson asked breathless while she fanned her face with a dainty lace handkerchief and looked at Winn with some uncertainty. The short jaunt from next door in the humidity caused the plump woman to perspire and become slightly winded.

"I'm okay," Winn said, desperately trying to curb her exasperation toward our well-meaning intervention.

"Well, I brought you some chicken soup that I had made for Moses yesterday, and a little peach cobbler," Mrs. Jackson said.

"You didn't have to do that, Miss Ida," Winn said, biting her lower lip.

I observed with some amusement that most southern women seemed to have adopted the absurd notion that food heals all illnesses. I gave a wry smile toward my sister who was obviously frustrated by all of the attention.

"Well, after you eat you should lie down for a while." Mrs. Jackson continued as if Winn had not said a word. She displayed a lovely smile with perfect white teeth and a rosy blush on her peachy cheeks, from which she was now dabbing moisture with the white handkerchief.

"Why is everyone telling me to lie down? I'm fine, really I am," she said with some irritation. It was an obvious battle of wills.

"Regardless as to whether you feel fine or not I want you to get some rest," Gran demanded. "If you don't want to go upstairs, you can stretch out here on the sofa.

"But I..." Winn was about to dig in her heels and launch into a full defense but when she saw the determined looks that the three of us gave her, she knew that to argue would be futile. She eased her petite frame back onto the sofa, reached for the remote control, yanked the coverlet over her, and yielded to the three unmovable forces that were not going to allow her to win this battle.

CHAPTER SEVEN

As a dream comes when there are many cares…

Ecclesiastes 5:3 (NIV)

12:03 a.m. Monday, June 10, 20__

Hard rain pummeled my window in a frenzied savagery that seemed to overtake the room. Exaggerated shadows from trees that danced wildly in the tempest formed grotesque shapes and figures on my bedroom walls as sleep transported me through a journey of disoriented imagery. My dreams were as tumultuous as the torrential storm that raged outside my bedroom. I tossed as a foggy mist enveloped my sleeping imagination and carried me to an enigmatic, yet familiar place I had often visited in my dreams.

In the dream, I was crouching, hiding under a blue and white net from a Huntsman. I heard a deafening clap of thunder that startled and shook me, but the rain never came. I heard the high shrill of a bird in the distance that reverberated like a hollow echo on the air, and then another thunderous boom. Then I heard the heavy footsteps of the Huntsman running toward me. I crouched still further underneath the heavy net, hoping that he would not see me hiding there. The footsteps stopped abruptly. Through the mist, I saw giant black, gray, and green birds that grouped together like pieces of a puzzle, but when the pieces came together, there was no distinguishable picture. The Huntsman was near, but I could not see his face. I held my breath for fear that he might hear me. There was a sudden growl that shook the ground where I crouched, but I could not see the animal. Soon the roar of the animal faded away into some far distant place. The Huntsman disappeared with it deep into the night.

An ear-splitting burst of thunder woke me from my dream, and I sprang upright from my sleep, confused because the sound of thunder seemed so real in my dream. I breathed deeply, trying to gather my thoughts. Another startling boom of thunder confirmed that I was no longer dreaming. It was pouring rain, and a flash of lightning flicked like a lashing whip outside my window.

I never liked storms.

I always hated the sound of thunder, and for the life of me, I never could make sense of my dread of the noise. I mean, I've always understood the science of what occurs to cause the blast, but for some reason I never could shake my unnatural fear of the sound. I know my fear is irrational, at least that's what I tell myself; but, I can still remember times when I was younger, and I would literally break out in a cold sweat because I was so terrified of the sound.

I looked out from my bed and watched as a dim street lamp below, revealed rivulets of rain sprinting down my window like streaks of liquid light. The muted blue-green light from my digital clock showed that it was 12:06 a.m.

"Good grief," I muttered. "I'm not going to be fit for anything in the morning." I pulled the coverlet back over my head and rolled over on my side. I drew my knees up to my chest under the blanket and sighed.

The dream still haunted me, after all this time. It still stalked me like a phantom, moving in and out of the murky shadows of my mind. Sometimes, I could go for months, even years without having the dream, but lately it has come with some frequency. But, why now?

I sat up in bed and laid my head against the headrest to watch as the wind hurled the rain mercilessly against my window. I reached for the pain reliever and glass of water that were next to my bed. My head still throbbed. I had decided to go to bed early after I developed a headache during dinner. I took a couple of pills and a sip of water, hoping the dull thud would subside. I grimaced, remembering that I was still quite annoyed with Grayson for contributing to my present discomfort. I could have cheerfully throttled him this evening!

I had called him after we had helped Winn to settle down. I asked if he wanted to come over and have Sunday dinner with us. Sundays were often busy for Grayson because he usually scheduled open house showings. He said that he would come after his last client. I puttered around the kitchen with Gran, pinching this and tasting that, until he arrived and she chased us both out of her kitchen so she could finish cooking.

Grayson and I had decided to take a walk around the neighborhood, and Winn coaxed Gran into letting her sit on the front porch so that she could get a little fresh air before the rain came.

Before I Wake

The intermittent clouds gathered like huge, soft, gray-white mountains that inched sleepily across the cerulean sky. Grayson held my hand as we walked with no particular destination in mind. We waved to friends who were out in patio chairs on their front porches, stopped and spoke with a few neighbors that had known us both as children, and chatted with those that had not seen Grayson for some time. Magnolia trees that were scattered throughout the neighboring streets flaunted the scent of their blossoms, and I breathed in the heady aroma that danced on the air. It was still humid, but an occasional breeze blew and teased the atmosphere with the light, westerly, winds that would eventually bring the rain.

I listened attentively while the boyishly handsome man who always had a ready smile, talked about the houses he had shown that afternoon. Grayson was clean-shaven with strong even features, and he wore his hair cut close to his head. His deep, brown, contemplative eyes reflected a restful patience that seemed infused within him. It made him approachable and seemingly unflappable.

Tailored, navy trousers covered long, strong legs that walked with ease up the slight incline that was the turning point of our jaunt, which directed us back toward home. Large, brown hands with lean fingers stretched into strong muscular arms that showed from underneath the upturned sleeves of an impeccably white, starched, cotton shirt. Those lean muscles now flexed as he pointed to show me a striking, red cardinal, perched on a creamy white magnolia blossom in a tree across the street.

Grayson seemed to possess a benevolent quality that appeared to place him above petty contrivances. I had often wondered if he might have inherited that quality from one of his parents. He was a solid, rational, good-natured man, who was as intelligent as he was engaging. I understood that he would always be a source of strength for me and that he would always be there for me, just as I would be there for him.

I sighed wistfully as we made our way back to the house.

I also understood that he wanted something more in our relationship. He wanted something lasting, and I knew that it meant putting down solid roots; roots that I knew I was not ready to plant. I, on the other hand, wanted to meet people, exchange new ideas, and see the world before I started a family. I had even thought about opening a small dance studio, and I had saved a considerable sum toward that end. I also knew that Winn and my grandmother both were cheering for Grayson. However, I was not going to be pushed into a relationship with him when I was not ready to take on such a great responsibility.

We had walked around the neighborhood for about an hour before we found our way back to the house. When we returned, Winn was still sitting on the porch reading. Gran was just inside the screen door when we stepped up on the porch.

"We were starting to wonder where you two were," Gran said. "I just finished putting dinner out on the table."

"You knew we wouldn't be that far from the house, Miss Mary," Grayson said, smiling at her.

"I thought you might have run off with this granddaughter of mine to marry her," she smiled.

"Gran..." I flushed, feeling a small knot in my stomach. The older woman chuckled and winked at Grayson.

"I wish," he winked back at her and gave her an impish grin.

"Dinner's ready. Go and wash up," she requested.

"Yes ma'am," we all said, in unison, and the three of us followed her inside for dinner.

We gathered for the Sunday feast in the dining area, which was an extension of the living room. Gran always cooked enough to feed a small army. She had made fried chicken, turnip greens, candied yams topped with marshmallows, cornbread, sweet tea, and a lemon pound cake for dessert.

"Miss Mary, you've outdone yourself," Grayson said with enthusiasm, and kissed her on the cheek, as he wheeled her chair to the table, and helped her get comfortable before he took his seat.

"Oh, go on with your sweet self! You're just a charmer." She gave a girlish giggle and beamed with delight at the compliment. "I can see why Souline is so crazy about you."

"Gran-n-n-n," I whined with embarrassment. Winn grinned and gave a slight chuckle at my discomfort.

"Is she now?" Grayson raised an eyebrow and studied me with an impudent regard. I frowned and shifted in my seat under his gaze. "Well maybe you can tell me how to win her over," his eyes were dancing with mischief.

"Oh, I think you've won her over. I just think you need to give her time to sort out a few things that's all. She'll eventually come around," Gran assured him with a chuckle and gave him still another wink.

Annoyed by all of the banter, I jumped to my feet and protested, "Just open up and swallow me now!" I pleaded with some unknown force to answer my petition and rescue me from the verbal torture that I felt was being meted out unfairly.

Surprised by my rather melodramatic outburst, the three cohorts glanced around the table at each other and gave an uproarious eruption of laughter. Realizing how ridiculous I must have looked standing there, I sat back down and crossed my arms over my chest in defiance. I looked at all of the food on the table and wished that there was an empty spot where I could lay my head.

"It's not funny!" I bemoaned, my accusatory glare shifting to each of them. "It's not funny!" I repeated, and suddenly a treacherous giggle that bubbled into uncontrollable laughter spilled from somewhere deep inside of me in spite of my discomfort.

"Well, I wish you two would hurry and do something," Winn said, still smiling.

"Don't you start," I reproached her, rolling my neck and eyes still laughing at the absurdity of the conversation.

"All I'm saying is that I want to be an aunt before I'm too old to appreciate being one," Winn laughed.

"What is this, *Pick-on-Souline-Day*?" I retorted as I looked around the table trying to control a smile that still twitched at the corners of my mouth.

"No, but..." Winn started.

"No, no, no! No more or I will take my food and eat out on the front porch. Alone!" I threw up my hands in self-defense to stave off the next barrage of hints and innuendo.

"Alright, I guess we've done enough damage," Winn chuckled and wrinkled her nose at me. "Besides, it's clouding up outside and we don't want you to get water logged."

"Humph!" I said, still smiling. "Thanks," I added dryly.

"Let us bow our heads." My grandmother smiled and said, and the mood shifted to a quiet reserve as each head lowered, and all eyes closed. "Lord, thank you for this time of love and family and truly for the bounty that you have set before us, that we may be nourished to do your work here on earth and that it will be to your glory. Amen."

"Amen," we each repeated.

The thunderous clouds, ushered in by the westerly wind had finally settled on top of Summerville like a mournful choir that murmured a lament in the distance and was threatening to deliver powerful aria for a climatic crescendo.

"It seems like we're having more and more storms these days," I observed. The tone of the company seemed to take on a more somber quality with the first waves of the inclement onslaught.

"I think that it's global warming," Grayson said, as he bit into a fried chicken leg with fervor.

"You can call it what you want to, baby," my Grandmother said. "But I think that it's a sign of the times. Pastor Martin was just saying this morning that a lot of the catastrophic weather we're experiencing is because we're living in the last days."

I stifled a groan and wondered why everything had to come back to religion.

"Well, scientists say that the greenhouse effect has a great impact on the condition of the earth's atmosphere," he added.

"Baby, no matter what they call it, the earth is still a living instrument of the Lord's, and the Bible speaks of disasters during our final days on earth," Gran stated rather matter-of-fact, as she placed more sliced tomatoes on his plate.

"Yes ma'am, but..." Grayson started, and I gently tapped his foot under the table and gave a slight shake to my head, as if to say, "Don't pursue this line of conversation."

"I know you young people think that you have all of the answers," she said, her sharp eyes staring over the rim of her glasses, noting the telling look I had just given Gray. "And, I know you think that a lot of the things that an old woman like myself might think are foolish. But, Grayson baby, God is real, and like I said, the earth is one among many of the instruments that he uses for his divine purposes." Grayson ignored my warning and continued the discussion.

"Yes ma'am, but I just don't understand how your God can allow these catastrophes to occur for his divine purpose." My insides began to knot up as he spoke. "I mean," Gray continued, "If God is as caring as you say he is, how could he just stand by and allow disastrous things to happen?"

"Well, Grayson, many of these occurrences are brought on by the violence of mankind," Winn intervened.

"I'm sorry, I don't get that," his brow furrowed and he gave a slight shake of his head. "What do you mean?" he asked, absently stroking his chin with his hand as if intrigued by the comment.

"Well, there is a scripture in Leviticus that speaks of the land vomiting out its inhabitants if they defile themselves. And in my opinion, this indicates that the land reacts to our sins.

"So..." he ruminated, "You think that there is some correlation between man's sins and the natural violent occurrences of the earth?" He asked, perplexed and with a hint of surprise.

"Yes, I do," she stated solemnly with a nod.

"I just don't see that. How did you reach such a conclusion?" Grayson asked. A spark of light danced in his eyes, and I knew that his interest had been piqued.

I cut my eyes in his direction, desperately trying to get his attention so that I could get him to drop this line of questioning. However, he had become intrigued with the direction of the conversation, and I understood him well enough to know that he loved a good debate, just like he loved a good book. It was like dangling catnip in front of a cat. I also understood Winn enough to know that she, just like Gray, was not about to let the conversation dissolve into nothing.

"A good example of this is when God allowed the flood to take place during the time of Noah, because of sin and the violence of men on the earth," Winn said quietly.

"So-ooo," Grayson continued smoothly and much to my dismay, "If we stop our sins the earth will respond favorably, and we would not be facing global warming?" He gave a little impudent chuckle.

"It sounds simplistic, I know," Winn conceded, disregarding his insolence. "Some of the destruction is our fault. We have mishandled the earth as well. We've been careless with our car emissions, our trash and dumped toxic waste into our waterways just to mention a few things. I'll admit we've done our share of damage. But, in answer to your question, it's not so much that the earth would respond favorably if we gave up our sins, but rather, God would bless us more favorably for honoring him by doing what's right."

"I see...," he seemed to weigh what she was saying. "Well let me ask you another question," he continued.

"Gray...," I glared at him. He had propelled the debate forward with his questions, and it began to gather energy like the storm that was gathering outside. I had an overwhelming urge to slap him.

Instead, I placed my hands to my temple as I started to experience the beginnings of a tension headache. He hesitated for a split second when he noticed the look of aggravation I had shot him.

"Are you alright?" asked my grandmother, who had not said a word during the verbal exchange.

I simply nodded to imply yes.

"Go ahead," Winn prompted Gray and looked at me as I lowered my head in my hands. I was familiar with the determined look that had settled on my sister's features and knew that this wasn't going to bode well.

There was a flash of lightning and the lights in the house flickered. A tremendous boom of thunder seemed to explode on top of the house. We each reacted with a little start at the unexpected sound. My nerves were starting to fray, and I was not sure if the cause was the storm outside that was brewing or the one that was gathering between Gray and Winn. I knew that Winn and Grayson's religious views were so vastly different that this conversation was about to plunge into a realm of no return. They had grabbed the proverbial *bone of contention* between their teeth, and neither was about to let go. In spite of my dissatisfaction, I watched Grayson and Winn with a resigned fascination and marveled at each of them for having entered into this discourse. Each flew headlong into the verbal tempest with views so diametrically opposed to the other it was like watching a skiff floating into a hurricane knowing that the results were not going to be favorable.

"Let's just say, for argument's sake, that what you're saying is true," he pursued. "Then why isn't this considered hell on earth? I mean with all of the chaos, violence, and unrest, there are people who already believe that this is hell."

Winn had propped her elbow on the table and placed her chin in her hand. She was speaking with an easy grace, but her eyes betrayed her calm. Flashes of her fervor were evident in those dark brown eyes, as it always was when she spoke about her faith in God.

"Well, this can't be hell," she said, "because hell is a place that is reserved for those who have not accepted Jesus Christ as their Savior." Grayson was now totally engrossed in the conversation. It was like reading a new novel that he could not put down.

"Now see that's what I don't get!" he exclaimed, his enthusiasm obvious. "What has my accepting or rejecting your Christ, got to do with me going to hell? For years, I've heard this stuff, but I've never understood how this one man, could keep me from going to hell. What's that about?" he queried, a dubious expression crossed his features.

Winn sat up in her chair and leaned forward to make her point. "Jesus Christ came to restore us to God."

"What?" Grayson said, obviously puzzled.

Winn offered a patient smile and said, "When Adam sinned through disobedience to God in the *Garden of Eden*, we became spiritually separated and lost to our spiritual God. Sin had tainted our true spirits. But Jesus Christ, the Son of God who *never* sinned, gave himself as a living sacrifice on our behalf, on the cross to restore our spirits to God. The only way that we can be redeemed to a holy, sinless, and righteous God is by accepting that Christ shed holy blood to cleanse us of our sins. This is why we refer to him as the *Sacrificial Lamb of God* for mankind," she stated quietly but emphatically.

"But, how does that keep us from going to hell? I mean, I know that Jesus existed, there's far too much literature on the man to refute his existence. I also know that he was considered to be a Jewish prophet, who performed, shall we say a number of questionable works." Winn slowly lifted her eyebrow at his reference to Christ's miracles.

"I just don't get how this guy, of all guys born on earth, can keep me from going to hell."

"Well, Grayson..." Winn's eyes flared with memory as she began to search through her mind for answers. "I know that it's difficult for a lot of people to grasp this concept because things that are accepted by faith are done so with the heart and not the head. But, just because you don't see air, doesn't mean that it does not exist, right?"

Grayson, stretched his legs out in front of him, folded his arms across his chest, and gave a tiny nod in agreement. "Well, God gave us each the gift of free will. We can either accept, of our free will, the gift that Christ died for our sins to restore us to God, or we can reject the idea and the gift of salvation through Christ. When God created mankind, he made us in his physical and spiritual image. Satan deceived Adam and Eve by telling them that they would not die if they ate from the *Tree of the Knowledge of Good and Evil*. Granted, they did not literally fall down and die at the very moment that they disobeyed God and ate from the tree. But, what Satan did not tell them is that they would begin to die and decay both physically and spiritually. Man was created to live forever, but the moment they ate from that tree, and because of their disobedience, sin entered the world and they were separated from God's spiritual fellowship. Since Satan deceived them, the whole world suffers in sin. The minute we are born, we start to die. We are born into sin because we are all Adam's children, and we are now spiritually separated from God as well.

Jesus, who is God's only son, was human born without sin, and he was given to the world as a gift to restore us spiritually to God, because we are sinful, and we are not spiritually clean enough to redeem ourselves to God. If we don't accept the gift, we will live spiritually separated from God forever, which is why we have hell," Winn explained.

Gray asked, "Which brings me back to my original question. If God is such a caring and loving God, why on earth would there even be a hell? I mean, if we have the gift of free will, as you say we do, and we decided not to go through all of this Jesus business, why do we have to endure hell for not accepting Him as part of our decision of free will? Why would a loving and caring God allow a hell to be made for those who chose, out of free will, to reject him?"

"Why would you reject the gift of a God who loves you and cares about you enough to sacrifice his only son on your behalf?" Winn asked quietly. Grayson blinked, slightly taken aback by the answer but not daunted.

"I'm just saying, isn't that what free will is all about?"

"Yes, it is."

"So why would he punish us for choosing a different road."

"Because, each of us born on this earth have been literally given the choice of deciding our future destinies. When we choose not to accept Christ we're basically saying that we choose death over life. We deny ourselves the gift of life that God provided for pardoning our sins. We are saying that we wish to die and be separated from God."

"But, what if you're a good person," he continued. "I mean I don't go out of my way to hurt anyone and I try to live peaceably with most people. I think that I'm a pretty decent guy."

"Well, the Scriptures say that only God is good and that man, because of Adam, is born into sin. So, on the day that we're born into this world, our sins separate us from God. God cannot live with sin. Christ came into the world because God loved us so much that he gave us a way to live with Him. If you accept this gift, then you will escape hell and live with God in peace and love forever."

"I understand that, but..."

I got up from the table and took my plate into the kitchen while my sister and Grayson continued the discussion. It was like watching two trains on the same track rush toward each other, and I just couldn't bear to watch anymore. I could not believe that he had gotten into this stupid debate with Winn.

I leaned over the sink, took a deep breath, and ran water over the dish. I was so angry with him that I could have strangled him. As long as I had known Gray, he had never allowed himself to be drawn into one of these conversations. What on earth possessed him to do such a thing now? I was so engrossed in thought that I did not hear my grandmother when she came into the kitchen.

"Baby, are you all right?" Gran asked. I gave a little start and my head snapped up from the chore of running dish water.

"Yes, ma'am, uhm ...well, I just have a bit of a headache."

"Didn't care much for the conversation I see," she said, eyeing me over the top of her spectacles.

"Ma'am?" I queried, a little taken aback by the barb. I looked at her warily because I was not used to sarcasm from my Grandmother.

"Souline, baby, you have got to stop running away from things. You've been doing that ever since your mother died."

"Oh Gran, you always say that. Besides I'm not running, I just get tired of the rhetoric."

"Rhetoric? Is that what you're calling it now? Rhetoric?" She stiffened a little but chose to let what she considered an insult pass. "Baby," she said patiently and spoke quietly to me as if I were a three-year-old who did not know any better. "We're living in the last days of this old earth, and I want you to start to see this world for what it truly is."

"Gran, please," I said impatiently, not wanting to get into this discussion now. My head was beginning to pound in earnest. "Can we please talk about something else? Can we just let it go?"

"No!" She snapped, and my head shot up, because of the unfamiliar sharpness in her voice. "I will not just let it go. I know in the past I have said that your salvation is your choice. But lately I've been troubled in my spirit about the way things are going in this world and quite frankly, this uneasiness I'm feeling has me a little worried. In the Bible, it talks about how during the last days, men will become lovers of themselves, covetous, thankless, unholy, without natural affection, lovers of pleasure more than lovers of God."

A haunted look that I had never seen before settled behind Gran's piercing brown eyes. Something urgent, almost desperate that made me wonder what had fueled her agitated behavior. "Every day we see on the news just how this prophecy is being fulfilled," she continued. "There's not a day that goes by where we don't hear of people robbing and murdering, mothers and fathers killing their children, husbands and wives killing each other, and then turning the guns on themselves. Souline honey, look around you, this world has become an ugly place for folks to live in."

I stared unseeing at the floor and did not say anything. There was nothing that I could say. There wasn't a day that had passed by that I hadn't found myself wondering about my own mother's death and why she had been murdered.

"Grayson just asked," she said, "'Why isn't this hell on earth?'

Before I Wake

Well, there's going to come a time on earth when the things that are happening now are going to seem like a picnic. I don't want a granddaughter whom I dearly love to face the horrible things that are going to happen after Jesus takes His believers from this earth. There is a sense of...of what I would call *expectancy* that I've started to feel lately. Something that I can't quite explain, and I don't know how much time we have left before Christ comes back to collect His children. All I know is that I just don't want you and Grayson left here to face the horrors that I know are coming."

"You're talking about the Rapture and the Tribulation aren't you?" I asked wearily.

Gran moved her wheelchair closer and took my hand. "Yes, I am. Baby, I love you and Grayson both, and I know that you think that I'm always preaching to you. But I don't want you to be left on this earth after the children of God are gone. Unimaginable disasters are going to occur on earth, and you won't be able to run then baby. There won't be anywhere for you to run or hide. The antichrist will rule the earth for a short period and no one will be able to escape. I don't want you to be alone. I mean, I don't want you to be left without God."

I looked at my Grandmother and released a slow even breath. My frustration was evident, but I was unable to express how I felt. I had grown up listening to my grandparents and others speaking about end time events since I was a child. I had heard about the wars, and rumors of wars, earthquakes, famines, pestilence, people with unnatural lusts, and quite frankly, I was just tired of it all. If the ground would truly open up and swallow me right now just to have it all over with I would be eternally grateful, I thought.

"Gran, I'm tired. I'm so tired." I fought back the tears that welled up in my eyes and threatened to spill over. I could hear the sound of the rain as it fell outside of the kitchen window and thought how fortunate for the sky to be able to shed her tears.

"I know you're tired," she said and patted my hand again. "But the tiredness you feel has more to do with the heavy load that you've carried in your heart since your mother died. You just need to let it go, baby." I sighed, knowing that there was some truth in what she said. The tiredness that had settled in my spirit was an old weariness that had been with me for some time. I'd never really been able to rid myself of the heaviness that I'd carried in my heart.

"I'll be alright, Gran." I hedged and pushed the door open to return to the dining room when she released my hand.

"I just hope it's not too late," she said, as she watched me move into the living room.

The debate had blossomed into a full-fledged war of words. Not heated and angry, but both seemed to delight in the sparring match they had entered into as they bobbed and parried in the verbal battle.

My headache had now developed into a migraine, and I finally dismissed myself and retreated to the peace of my bedroom. They were so engrossed in the skirmish that they barely knew that I had left the room. However, I did notice that I left under the scrutiny of my grandmother's keen, watchful eyes as I ascended the stairs.

Now, as I sat up in bed and listened to the storm outside my window, my grandmother's words reverberated in my ears. *'But, I don't want you to be left on this earth after the children of God are gone.'* The words floated to the surface of my mind like a bubble in a bottle. *'The tiredness you feel has more to do with the heavy load that you've carried in your heart since your mother died. You just need to let it go..., just need to let it go..., just need to let it go...'* The words resounded like an echo that whispered over and over in my head and pierced my heart each time that it did. I hugged my knees to my small frame and allowed the tears that I could not release earlier that evening to fall.

Why did I always feel so tired in my spirit? Why did I always feel so empty inside? Why did it always feel as though I was fighting some unknown battle? A dozen other *why's* ran through my mind as I stared unseeing at the ceiling that was occasionally being lit by vivid flashes of lightning from outside my window.

Desperate for sleep, I closed my eyes against the raging storm only to contend with my subconscious in a fitful storm of my disquieted rest. When I finally drifted off to sleep the last thing I remembered asking was...

"Why?"

CHAPTER EIGHT

When wilt thou arise out of thy sleep?

Proverbs 6:9 (KJV)

6:15 a.m. Monday, June 10, 20__

I woke to an irritating buzz that finally registered to my drowsy, sluggish, mind as my alarm clock sounding its morning hymn. I squelched an overwhelming impulse to pull the annoying intermeddler out of the wall and throw it out into the hallway. Instead, I smacked the button with more vigor than was necessary to stop the annoying sound. It was still raining, but not with the raging fury of the night before. I sat up on the side of my bed yawned, stretched my arms above my head, and then placed my head in my hands.

"I feel like death warmed over," I moaned, as I noticed that the dull throb of my headache had not completely relinquished its grasp. I yawned once more, tugged at my pink night top, and padded toward the bathroom to perform my morning rituals and prepare for work.

By the time I finished my breakfast, my headache still had not lifted, and I felt slightly sluggish from my lack of sleep.

Winn had deemed it necessary to give me a blow-by-blow of the conversation she and Grayson had gotten into last night after I left. She had found his views extremely interesting. She also proceeded to tell me of her concerns about both Grayson's and my salvation and said that she would like to talk us when we could find the time.

I laid my head on the kitchen table and moaned. I really was not up to teaching class today. I thought that it would be nice to stay home and sleep and that I would feel much better if I could get rid of the headache that still lingered. However, I was grateful to escape the lecture that I was about to get when I heard the familiar car horn that announced Grayson's arrival. It helped me to decide that I had better make the effort to go into work. I grabbed my belongings and headed out the door.

The steady rain bounced like high-spirited acrobats on the bright red umbrella that I unfurled to shield myself as I hurriedly walked to the car to meet Grayson. I gracefully dodged small puddles on the walkway as he came around to open the car door for me. I grunted to indicate my thanks and hurried into the car to escape the steady downpour.

"Good morning," he said cheerfully, shaking the water from his umbrella before tossing it onto the floor in the back of the car and sliding himself into the car next to me.

"Good morning," I condescended, unable to rise to his cheerful greeting.

"Are you okay?" he continued. "You look a little sleepy."

"Do I?" I asked irritably.

"What's wrong? Did you get up on the wrong side of the bed?" He gave a small chuckle and nudged me in the side with his elbow as he steered the car onto the road.

"No thanks to you," I muttered under my breath.

"Excuse me?" he tossed a glance my way as he maneuvered past a huge puddle that spilled across the road.

"Forget it," I responded peevishly and frowned.

"What's with you?" he said observing this time, that I looked more aggravated than tired.

"What's with me?" I snapped, unable to suppress my irritation. "What's with me is the fact that you got into that ridiculous conversation with my sister last night. That's what's with me! What were you thinking, Gray?"

"What's wrong with that?" he asked, surprised at my outburst. "I enjoyed talking with your sister last night. It was interesting listening to her views about her religion. I didn't think that..."

I cut him off, "That's just it. "You didn't think!" I flung the words at him. "You start a battle like that, but I'm the one left floundering in the aftermath of the clash."

"What are you talking about, Souline?" He extinguished a small flare of temper and gave an audible sigh instead.

I glared at him, "I'm talking about the lectures that I got, first from my grandmother about my salvation, and another one this morning at breakfast from Winn. You were able to go home and sleep like a baby I bet if that cheerful disposition of yours is any indication of your luck. Whereas, I was up half the night tossing and turning with a wretched headache. You knew very well, from our conversation at breakfast yesterday, that I'm fed up to here," I raised a hand above my head for emphasis, "of the *religious-speak* that I'm spoon fed daily. But, No-oooo, you had to bring it up again. And now you have the nerve to ask me if I got up on the wrong side of the bed!" I heatedly spat out the words, my breast heaving with anger.

We approached the empty parking lot of a law firm that had not opened for the day's business, and he guided the car toward the empty spaces and parked.

"Look, Souline," he said, turning toward me and quelling his irritation when he realized that he was the cause of my distress. "I-I never intended to start a fight between you and your family. You know that I would never do that," he said contritely. "It's just that I've never really sat and talked to them about their religious views."

"So why on earth did you decide to last night?" I exploded, angrily and slightly bewildered by his actions.

"I've been curious about them for a while," he admitted. "I wanted to know," he said honestly.

"And you've known my family for how long?" I drawled, my voice dripping with sarcasm.

He allowed the comment to pass. "Souline, honey you know that I would never deliberately cause you any pain, and I'm sorry if I have now. I just got caught up in the conversation with Winn before I knew it. Believe me when I say that I meant you no harm." I held the gaze that reflected an earnest apology behind his dark brown eyes.

"However," he continued, "I do know of a way to solve the problem you have with your family." I folded my arms across my chest and glared at him, not quite ready to relinquish my anger.

"Oh, really? Amaze me." I said, with some acerbity.

"You can make your home with me," he said, in such a nonchalant manner that you would have thought he had just asked me out for a cup of coffee. "That way you can avoid most of these confrontations with your family," he continued, with no indication of frivolity in his voice or his manner.

I was so caught off guard that my mouth flew open. I was bereft if breath and I blinked nonplused. I stared at him with such an incredulous expression that I knew that I must have appeared quite comical, and was so dumbfounded that I was not quite sure what to say next. I closed my mouth, opened it again, and then settled on closing it once more.

"Souline?" He turned in his seat to face me with sincerity etched on his boyishly handsome face, his imploring eyes searching for an answer.

When I finally found my voice, I faltered and made a noise that sounded almost like I was clearing my throat. "Uhm, I uhm Gray...Grayson." I had totally drawn a blank. "I-I...uhm ..." I repeated foolishly. "We're going to be late for work," was all I could manage to say. I sounded stupid even to my own ears.

"I'm sorry, I really didn't mean to spring it on you this way," he absently ran a hand over his head a couple of times before he placed it back on the steering wheel.

"I mean," he hesitated slightly. "I-I wanted to ask you in a better way and in a much better setting. "Something..." he wavered, "you know...more romantic, and certainly for a much better reason than avoiding conversations with your family."

"That's okay," I spoke quietly, staring down at my hands, and trying to find words to ease the tension that had grown exponentially and invaded the tiny space. "We're going to be late," I repeated almost inaudibly, my mind leaping in a hundred different directions.

He nodded in agreement not quite sure what to say either. I got the impression that he did not want to press the subject. I guess he realized that sitting in the rain, in a car, in an empty parking lot was hardly a place to talk about our future.

The rain persisted as he eased the car back into the morning traffic and steered the car in the direction of the school. We continued the remainder of the way in an uneasy silence. I did not want to find myself staring at him, so I placed my head on the rest and closed my eyes. To be honest, I was tired enough to fall asleep, but after the bomb that was just dropped in my lap, I could not have slept if I had wanted to. Grayson concentrated on driving and did not utter another word until he helped me out of the car with the promise of picking me up after school.

When I got out of the car, my mind was whirling. My headache had returned full force, and I really didn't want to think about the conversation we had just had.

When the morning classes began, I threw myself into my work with more zeal than usual. Summerville School of Performing and

Creative Arts was a year round school, where I taught ballet and modern dance. This morning, I worked with an energy that I had not known that I possessed.

I had always been known for my rigorous practice sessions, and if I seemed more motivated than usual, no one dared to question my enthusiasm. I taught grades six through twelve, and I had never been more grateful in my life for the distraction my students provided me today.

It rained off and on the remainder of the day. Instead of grading student papers, or taking a walk around the campus during my free period, I sought solitude in the quiet of the school's auditorium. It wasn't used during this time of day unless there was a school assembly or a rehearsal for a performance in one of the other departments.

I walked in the cool, dark, room and allowed the quiet to wash over me like a soothing balm. My frazzled nerves seemed to heal in the peaceful atmosphere. The lights on the stage were dimly lit, and I threw my sweater over one of the chairs and walked up the side steps to reach the stage.

I positioned my feet and performed a series of stretches to warm my muscles. I placed my arms in *port de bras* and began to move languidly through each dance position. I skipped and fluttered across the stage, letting my mind take me to a place where I could freely and openly express my feelings through the movement of my body.

I danced through a series of movements as I imagined a place where I could see sound and hear color; a place where lights, music, and movement were one. I lost myself in the sights and sounds that flooded my imagination, and I moved around the stage into beautiful exotic places that only my dreams could take me. Then, all at once, I was aroused from my reverie for the second time by a rude sound. It was the sound of the bell telling me that that my free period had ended.

I was forced to step out of my dream world and back to the reality of pupils walking through the halls, locker doors being opened and slammed, and the sound of young voices echoing throughout the building.

My mind gradually returned to the real world, and I sighed, realizing that I had to leave my sanctuary to go to my next class. I slowly walked from the stage, seized my sweater from where I had tossed it over the empty chair, and walked back to my classroom studio to finish what was left of my school day.

By the time I reached home at the day's end, I was physically and emotionally drained. I was never so glad to see a place in my life.

On our ride home, I was pleasantly surprised and extremely grateful that Grayson did not broach the subject of our early morning conversation. He had talked about work and potential clients and new homes that had come on the market. In fact, I got the impression that he was doing his level best to avoid the topic. When he helped me out of the car, he gave me a quick peck on the cheek and said he would talk to me later.

I walked into the house, literally threw myself onto the living room sofa, and pulled the teal and white crochet coverlet over my body. I snuggled further down into the soft confines of the sofa, closed my eyes, and released a long, airy breath. I wanted to shut out the world even if it was just for a little while.

"Souline." My eyes flew open. "Baby, is that you?" The gentle query came from the general direction of the kitchen.

"Yes ma'am," I called back to Gran. "Do you need any help?" I asked, gnashing my teeth because in my heart I was unwilling to relinquish the comfortable spot I had just made for myself on the sofa if she answered, yes.

"No, sweetheart," Gran answered. I heard the soft whir of her electric wheelchair when she came into the room and stopped next to me and gave me a gentle pat on the arm. "Did you have a hard day?" She asked and leaned down and kissed my forehead.

"Umm, yes ma'am. I didn't sleep very well last night, because of the storm."

"You never have liked thunderstorms," she reflected. "Well after you eat, I want you to turn in early. You hear me?" she insisted.

"Yes, ma'am," I smiled and nodded obediently, letting her fuss over me as if I were a young child. The sweet hint of vanilla she always wore caressed my nose when she bent to kiss me on my cheek. She had just tucked the blanket under me and caressed one of my hands when the front door opened, and Winn walked inside.

"Hey!" she gave her customary greeting.

"Hey yourself," I said, without popping my up head from its comfortable resting place.

"Hey, Gran." Winn grinned and kissed the top of her head and looked down at me resting on the sofa.

"What's wrong with you?" She asked with a chuckle. "Too

much Grayson last night?"

"Yes, thanks to you," I gently reproached her.

She chuckled again and asked, "What's that supposed to mean?" She absently reached for the remote resting near where she placed her handbag on the coffee table. She eased my feet back so that she could share the sofa with me.

"Nothing," I said.

"I think that he asked some very valid questions last night," Winn continued while she flicked through the channels.

"Just let it go," I insisted. I really didn't want to get into another war of words that might lead to another sermon about my soul's salvation.

Gran wheeled back into the kitchen where we heard her rattling earthenware.

"Alright, I'll let it go, but I do want to talk to you when you feel up to it. Okay?"

"Okay," I agreed quickly, simply because I was drained. I was going to ask her what she wanted to discuss, but I was tired, and I was not in the mood for a full-blown debate, so I was glad to let the subject drop.

"Well, I've got to get ready," Winn patted my feet and stood up.

"Where are you going?" I asked when she picked up her belongings and started up the stairs. We were in the habit of watching television until Gran called us to eat dinner.

"I've got a choir rehearsal this evening. The church is having an anniversary concert, and I'm playing most of the music. I've got to be ready by the end of next month. I want you and Grayson to come, too. You'll love it," she said and sprinted up the stairs as if she had just gotten her second wind.

"Aren't you going to eat?" I called after her.

"No, I'll eat later," she said and darted off.

I snuggled underneath the coverlet again and switched the television station to the news.

The words *Breaking News* scrolled across the screen as a well-groomed anchorman spoke to his television audience. "Here is what we have so far, there are confirmed reports stating that world leader, Hadrian Maxmillian, was pronounced dead at the scene when he was allegedly stabbed by Omar Mohammad who is believed to be a known terrorist leader."

I listened more intently, "Mohammad accused Mr. Maxmillian of undermining their Jihadist efforts by initiating the *New World Peace Treaty*. A treaty instituted to guarantee Israel as a sovereign state and maintain peace in Middle Eastern countries that have historically been plagued with the threat of terrorism, nuclear war, and armed conflicts. Mohammad was dragged away by secret police yelling to Mr. Maxmillian, Death to the Great Satan, after he allegedly stabbed the world leader in the head with a concealed weapon, as Mr. Maxmillian was entering his car Monday after leaving the Global Summit.

Mr. Maxmillian was one of one hundred thirty-nine world leaders attending the Global Summit in Rome, Italy. He was instrumental in establishing this New World Peace Treaty over three years ago.

Six other members of the terrorist network, who were detained for questioning along with Mohammad, had spent the past sixteen months working out the details of the attack on Mr. Maxmillian. Again, this is breaking news, and we will continue to issue updates as we obtain information. In other news..."

After I had heard Winn leave, the sound of the news reports diminished as my eyelids fluttered until I finally gave in to sleep. I was still tired from my lack of rest from the night before, and I slept for about thirty minutes before Gran woke me for dinner.

As I washed the dishes and tidied up the kitchen, I could hear Gran in the living room talking to her potted plants. There were a sundry of ivy plants, philodendrons, and dish gardens that were dispersed around the room. She pampered the beautiful green things as if they were small children in need of the love of a nurturing mother. I could hear her cooing to them like they were babies. After I had finished the dishes, I went upstairs to my room and graded the papers I should have graded earlier, took a shower, and climbed into bed.

All day long, I had desperately tried to push Grayson's offer from my mind. I had managed to subdue the thoughts earlier at work because my students had occupied my time. However, there was nothing to stem the mental tide from flowing now, and it kept creeping forward like slow-rising flood waters seeping under a closed door. The more I pushed to keep it out, the more persistent it became until there was a deluge. Grayson's offer was like a wave churning a sea of emotions inside of me.

What on earth was he thinking to have asked such a thing? Had Grayson lost his mind? He knew that I wasn't ready for marriage. Didn't he?

I had told him on more than one occasion that I wanted to save and open my own dance studio. He knew this. He knew that I want to travel and see other countries and meet new people. So why on earth would he even suggest marriage?

As I lay on the bed tossing and turning trying to allay this emotional tsunami that Grayson had set into motion, a thought suddenly occurred to me. He had not actually offered me marriage. My mind rushed back to the morning's conversation, and I recalled that he had actually said, '*You can make your home with me.*' Did he mean marriage or was he asking me to live with him? Surely he knew better than to ask me such a thing. But he hadn't actually come right out and asked, "*Souline, will you marry me?*" Had he? I just assumed that he meant marriage. Maybe he thought that because I wasn't ready to get married, that living with him would be an alternative solution. Surely he had sense enough to know that I was not going to play house with him.

A rush of hot anger seized me, and my mind went into a whirlwind of restless thoughts. I tried, but I could not shut off my mind.

I tossed and turned until I finally managed a tattered, restless sleep.

CHAPTER NINE

See, I am sending an angel ahead of you to guard you along the way.

Exodus 23:20 (NIV)

5:58 p.m. Monday, June 10, 20__

Winn slid the dark blue van into the parking space labeled Choral Director, turned off the ignition, gathered her purse and sheet music, and walked toward the side entrance of Pleasant View Baptist Church.

"Hello, Sister Thrasher, how's the concert coming along?" The congenial inquiry came from Pastor Martin, who was coming out of one of the Sunday school rooms just as she entered the side corridor.

"Oh, good evening, Pastor Martin, it's coming quite well, Winn said and bit her lip, and added, "I think," with a wry smile. His appearance often reminded her more of an elder statesman in his dark suits and bowties, than a pastor. He was a kind man with a quiet dignity and bright, discerning eyes.

His warmth and benevolence allowed him to look beyond the

outer qualities of an individual and enabled him to see what was not readily evident in one's character. His gift of discernment gave him the ability to assess someone's character before prematurely pronouncing judgment on that person. He guided the members of his church as if they were his children and not just members of his congregation.

During the twenty-eight years that he had served at Pleasant View, there had never been a breath of scandal about him or his lovely wife, Rachel, and together they embraced the congregation with goodwill, love, and compassion.

"Well, I'm glad," he smiled, and the perpetual twinkle in his eyes radiated a warmth that always put Winn at ease.

"I came in a little early so that I could practice a couple of songs before rehearsal," she explained.

"That's fine, that's fine." He patted her shoulder and trotted off down the hall. "I'll be in my office if you need me, young lady," he said over his shoulder and disappeared into the room.

The sanctuary, with its ivory-colored walls and royal blue, cushioned pews, had witnessed a multitude of hymns, prayers, and testimonials from the numerous members that had entered its doors over the years. The emptiness of the room contradicted the warmth and fullness of the lives that had been changed through christenings, baptisms, and even eulogies in the now uninhabited, sacred place. Stained glass windows depicting eight different scenes of Christ's mission on earth, starting with his birth and ending with his ascension into heaven, added a sense of reverence to this place of worship.

Winn looked around at the various brass and wooden religious artifacts that were interspersed around the room as she eased her petite figure onto the organ bench in the choir stand. She smiled feeling quite at home in this quiet place as she always did since her very first visit to the church.

It was not long after her mother had died when she and her sister attended their first church service at Pleasant View Baptist with their grandparents. She loved how friendly and caring everyone was at this church. She also loved how they seemed more like family than just people who showed up to say that they were on the church membership roll. At the age of sixteen, she gave her life to Christ, was baptized and she became a steadfast member of the church community. Whereas Souline's attendance diminished after their grandfather's death until she finally stopped going altogether.

While growing up in the church, Winn was often asked to play for church recitals, concerts, and special services. So when the former choral director, Sister Maxine Lawson, left to live with her sister up North, Pastor Martin asked Winn if she would be interested in playing for the youth choir permanently. She loved working with children, and she jumped at the chance. She agreed and became the youth choral director at the age of nineteen.

She smiled to herself again, as her dainty fingers ran across the keys of the enormous pipe organ, and she started to play the hymn, *Angels the First Born Sons of Light*. While she played, her eyes became transfixed on the stained glass window that had the representation of Christ's ascension into heaven.

There was a depiction of several angels on the earth and in the air. Winn's eyes were fixated on the angels as they seemed to move into and out to the frame of the window. The images became a vortex before her as if she was being carried into the picture itself among the angels. She felt as if she was being lifted from her seat and moved into a place that somehow seemed oddly familiar. The atmosphere seemed to swirl and shift in and out of time and space around her, very beautiful, very bright, white, and clear. Then just as suddenly as she entered into the ethereal sphere, she exited.

Everything went black.

7:23 p.m. Monday, June 10, 20__

I lifted my head from the pillow and looked at the clock to see that it had only been about an hour since I had tossed and turned into a fitful sleep when I overheard my Grandmother's agitated inquiries.

Voices floated upstairs into my bedroom from the floor below and broke into the muzzy light sleep I had achieved. I sat up on my elbow and realized that the agitation was concerning Winn. I hurriedly tugged on a pair of jeans and an old tee-shirt and charged down the flight of stairs to the living room, when I heard other unfamiliar voices mingling with my grandmother.

"What's wrong?" I asked, unconcerned about the niceties that were usually expected when someone enters a room.

A tall, medium-built, dark-skinned man with a sprinkling of gray hair that framed his temples blurted out, "We found her on the floor of the choir stand." He received a cutting look for his lack of tack from a rather attractive woman who appeared to be in her early forties, standing next to him.

"What?" I exclaimed as a wave of anxiety rushed through my body like a shock of electricity while I rushed toward my sister.

"Walter, really!" admonished the woman, who was dressed in an impeccable gray pleated skirt, with a pink *crêpe-de chine* blouse, and a gray silk scarf. A diamond and silver brooch held the scarf in place. Her countenance was quite elegant compared to the man that stood next to her. Not that he appeared to be dowdy, but he was dressed in comfortable jeans, sneakers and held a baseball cap in his hands.

"She had a little fainting spell is all, honey," she continued.

"This is Mr. and Mrs. Sterling, two of our church members. Brother Sterling drives our church bus on Sundays," Gran said, by way of offering quick introductions. I nodded my acknowledgments and offered a slight smile. "Mrs. Sterling insisted on driving Winn home from choir rehearsal, and Mr. Sterling drove our van so that it wouldn't be left in the church parking lot overnight."

"You fainted, again?" I said to her, my anxiety heightened at this news.

"Again?" Mr. Sterling's head shot up. "Sandra, maybe we should have taken her to the hospital like I said in the first place," Mr. Sterling complained.

"Honestly, Walter," his wife poked him in his side with a long, shiny red, fingernail and shot him a slightly exasperated look.

"Winn, what happened?" I demanded. "What caused you to faint?"

"Well, I'm not really sure. I do remember that I got to the

church a little before six o'clock and parked. I gathered my belongings from the van and talked to Pastor Martin for a moment. I went into the sanctuary and started practicing one of the hymns that we're going to sing for the concert...," she hedged a little, as if she was carefully considering her words, and then finally said, "and... the next thing I remembered is Sister Sterling helping me up off the floor."

"Maybe you should let us take you to the hospital," Mr. Sterling reiterated.

"No, really," Winn held up a hand to stop him. "I'm alright. Now that I'm home, I'll be fine."

"Winn, that's not a bad idea. You've never fainted before in your life," I reminded her. "But this is the second time in two days that this has happened. I don't like this," I said, trying to keep the anxiety from rising in my voice.

"No now, I draw the line at going to the hospital. Really, I'm okay," she said firmly. "Brother and Sister Sterling thank you for bringing me home," Winn continued. "I appreciate your kindness, but I think that all I need is a good night's rest. Gran and Souline will take care of me," she said to the visitors as a polite way of dismissing her guests and ending the conversation.

"It won't be a problem for us to take you to the hospital," Mr. Sterling insisted as his wife rolled her eyes heavenward and tugged on his arm to move him toward the door.

"Baby, maybe Brother Sterling and Souline are right," Gran spoke up.

"Gran, I'm just tired that's all," she said impatiently, casting eyes that entreated her to stifle the conversation. "I didn't eat dinner before I left and maybe that contributed to the spell."

"Yes, my brother has diabetes and when his blood sugar..." Mr. Sterling began.

"Walter!" Mrs. Sterling snapped and spoke more sharply than she obviously intended. She forced a smile and continued through clenched teeth. "Honey, maybe we should let her family take it from here."

"Well..." Gran said, with resignation in her voice. "If you're not feeling better in the morning you're going straight to the doctor. Do you hear me?"

"Yes, ma'am," Winn agreed, relieved that Gran had picked up on the signal and did not pursue the conversation any further.

However, I was not easily convinced and eyed her with some apprehension. I did not want to exacerbate the situation by insisting that she be taken to the hospital, but I was very concerned about her fainting spells. Despite her diminutive size, Winn had a hearty constitution. She was not prone to the infirmities and frailties that seemed to characterize the anatomies of some petite females. This was not to say that she had not been subject to an occasional cold or flu, but for the most part, she had passed most maladies without complaint. So the whole idea of her fainting caused me more than just a little concern.

Gran and I thanked the couple profusely for their kindness and waved goodbye to them as they walked to their car. As soon as they had driven off, I darted upstairs to Winn's room where I found her sitting on the edge of her bed staring down at her hands.

"Winn?" I said, and I moved hurriedly toward the bed. She was deep in thought, and her head snapped up when I called her name.

"Souline, please don't start. Honestly, I'm just not up to it; really I'm not. I'm fine," she pleaded, in one breath without pause.

"I'm not starting," I said, my feelings were a little bruised, but I ignored the comment when I noticed how tired she really looked. "I'm just concerned about you. That's all. You're my only sister you know."

"I know," she said quietly, grabbing my hand and pressing it against her cheek. "And I love you for it, but I'm convinced that it's nothing that a good night's sleep won't fix." She gently patted my hand and let it go. We heard the soft hum of Gran's wheelchair, as she came into the room.

"Are you okay, baby?" Gran asked, those piercing dark eyes searching Winn's face and noticing the signs of fatigue. "You look tired."

"Yes, ma'am. I was just telling Souline that I just need a good night's sleep, and I'll be fine."

"Well alright," Gran said, and reached over and hugged Winn. "If you're sure."

"I'm sure," Winn nodded her assurance. Gran smiled and turned the chair and wheeled herself down the hall to her bedroom. I also hugged her and allowed the conversation to cease. However, I made her promise that if she did not feel well by morning she would let us take her to the doctor. She hugged me again and agreed.

"Good night," I said. "If you need anything during the night just let me know, okay?"

Winn nodded and said softly, "Good night," as I walked toward the door and went into my room.

It was just a short while until I heard Winn and my Grandmother settle down to a quiet rest. However, I lay awake for some time considering what was causing Winn to have these fainting spells. Eventually, I managed to drift off, and the sleep that had eluded me earlier finally came.

CHAPTER TEN

They were eating and drinking and marrying.

Matthew 24:38 (KJV)

6:57 a.m. Tuesday, June 11, 20__

The town of Summerville woke to a beautiful summer day. The sky was a startling deep cerulean blue, and the intoxicating smell of the earth dallied on the breeze like a wink from a coquettish admirer. The malevolent storms and rain that had rattled the small southern town the day before were moving eastward where the much-needed rain was expected to break a four-month long heat drought in many of the northeastern states.

For weeks, temperatures had reached unseasonable record-breaking highs on the east coast, and the predicted rains were expected to bring cooler weather and offer some relief from the drought. Summerville's vegetation had been revitalized and was now releasing the exhilarating scent of freshly watered earth.

I felt refreshed this morning. I yawned and stretched, having opened my bedroom window so that I could breathe in the morning air. The dainty floral pattern of orange blossoms whirled around as I did a pirouette before I went into the bathroom to shower and got ready for school.

I sailed down the stairs toward the kitchen and was met with the delicious aroma of bacon, eggs, grits, toast, and coffee. Gran and Winn were already eating when I came into the kitchen. I hugged them both and eyed my sister with some regard.

"Are you okay this morning? How do you feel?" I asked Winn as I seated myself on the other side of Gran.

"Now don't you start, I just got through telling Gran that I feel great." She smiled, but I noticed the surreptitious glance that passed between the two of them that seemed to hint at the discussion that they shared before I came into the room. I didn't offer any comment for fear that it may lead to another debate on religion.

I took a bite of unbuttered wheat toast and a sip of coffee and saw that she honestly looked non-the-worst-for-wear and nodded my approval, although I still looked for tell-tale signs of fatigue, but there were none that I could see.

"Well, you look okay, but if you have another episode, Winn, we will make sure that you go to the doctor. Okay? And, no shilly-shallying from you." I insisted.

"Scouts' honor." Winn smiled as she held up three fingers saluted and then hugged me.

I sighed. I enjoyed mornings like this, the conversation was as bright and sunny as it was outside. We laughed and teased each other with love and grace. It was almost, always this way with my family. Everyone seemed happy to be in the other's company. Even when life proved to be a little trying at times, it was nice to know that this was a family that cared and would give anything just to make things a little more comfortable for the others, whenever possible.

I was having my second cup of coffee and laughing at something silly Winn had said when we heard a light tapping at the back door, and Gran immediately responded.

"Come on in, Ida!" Mrs. Jackson came in hauling a fairly oversized straw basket.

"Good morning! How's everybody?" she asked cheerfully, her plump cheeks tinged with color from handling the laden basket.

"Fine," the perfunctory answer was given from everyone at the table.

"What have you got there, Miss Ida?" Winn asked, having walked over to help her place the basket on top of the washing machine situated near the door.

"Oh, I brought over some yellow squash, turnip greens, and tomatoes that my Moses got from his garden," she puffed out. "I just stopped by for a minute." A telling look passed between Winn and me. We understood from years of experience that a minute usually meant the conversation between the two older women could reach marathon status.

"I intended to bring them yesterday, but Moses was having a little trouble with that hand of his. It's that arthritis of his, you know? You girls okay?" She said, in one breath. She ran her hands down the front of her immaculate floral apron to wipe away some imaginary dirt from it after she placed the basket down. I smiled at the gesture. Miss Ida was always as neat as a pin. I could not ever remember seeing the woman unkempt.

"Yes, ma'am," Winn said. "Why don't you take my chair, I'm on my way out."

"Here, let me get you some coffee," I offered and rose from my chair.

"Why, thank you, baby," she said to me and then turned to Winn and asked, "Are you feeling better?" Miss Ida sat down next to her friend and smoothed her hands over her apron again.

"Yes, ma'am," Winn answered quickly, for fear of drifting into deeper waters concerning the fainting spell she'd had last night that she did not care to share with their kind, but often overly inquisitive neighbor.

"How are things at that school of yours?" she asked, as I reached for a cup from the cabinet to pour her some coffee.

"Good," was all I managed to say before she turned to Gran and changed the subject so that there was no lull in the conversation.

"Oh girl, did you see the news this morning?" The plump lady looked appalled, remembering the news report she was about to elaborate on as she reached for a piece of toast that Gran offered. She smiled and nodded her thanks to Gran and then said, "Thank you, baby," when I returned with her cup of coffee.

Miss Ida sweetened her coffee with half a teaspoon of sugar and added a little bit of cream. I glanced patiently at the woman who always came bearing the tragedies of the morning news, and made my excuses as I removed my empty plate, cup, and utensils from the table and walked over to the sink.

"G-irlll, "she extended the word into a long slow drawl as she always did. "It's another, *I need to be on my knees praying as we speak* morning," she said to Gran.

I had quietly mouthed the exact words of our neighbor as she spoke, and Winn poked an elbow in my side and grinned at me for my insolence as we stood at the sink.

"Mary, g-irlll," she drawled again, "Did you see where that man...what's his name, Maxmillian was stabbed to death?"

"Honey, yes, I saw some of it," Gran responded, not to be outdone by her friend's observations. "The attacker just came out of nowhere and...," she snapped her fingers to indicate the violent act.

"I know," Miss Ida nodded. "I don't mean to speak ill of the dead, but something about that man always made me a little nervous. I don't know why. But well...," she allowed her voice to trail off. "People treated him like he's some kind of holy man that was going to lead the people to the Promised Land ever since he wrote that peace treaty. Quite frankly, I think he's the devil himself."

"Me too," Gran nodded in agreement. "I don't understand how people can get so caught up in other people's lives and believe the things that these ole' crazy people say. It's almost as if people can't think for themselves anymore these days," Gran returned emphatically.

Winn broke in, "Well, we'd better be off, or we're going to be late." We nudged and poked each other as we went out the room like two mischievous schoolgirls, and knew that if we stood there long enough we would be pulled into the morning's report. We left the ladies sitting at the kitchen table to indulge in their morning fill of gossip.

Winn assured me that she felt quite well when I inquired once more about her well-being, and gently pushed me toward the door when we heard the familiar toot of Grayson's car horn. I grabbed my tote bag that was on the sofa and walked out to the car.

The morning ride was pleasant. The conversation between us was light and easy as we drove toward school. We spoke of the expectations of the day that lay before us until he pulled up to the curb to let me out with the promise of picking me up after school and having dinner with me that evening. I smiled and waved goodbye as he drove off.

As I made my way through the hallway toward my studio classroom, I received an occasional 'Good morning, Ms. Thrasher,' from students who were in my dance classes.

I settled into my routine for the day and prepared to receive my students. I had decided the night before to give each class a pop quiz that was received with a disgruntled moan or two from a few students. I divided the students into small groups and each had ten minutes to devise an impromptu routine using any number of moves or positions that I had taught in class.

I was quite pleased with the overall performances of most of the students and made notes of some routines or positions that may need to be repeated or enhanced in class so that the students would have a better understanding of the methods. I also noted the students who needed a little more help and encouragement.

I loved teaching and was proud that I was able to pass this beautiful and creative art form on to my young charges. I loved the beauty and the grace of dance. It brought about a discipline and an awareness of the mind and body in a way that few art forms allowed. When I needed solace from the madness of the masses, it brought about a creative retreat that seemed to make the outside world disappear.

The day went by uneventfully, and I was grateful for the sound of the bell that indicated the school's workday had ended. I gathered my belongings and sat outside on the wrought iron bench situated near an old maple tree that had kept the secrets of many students and faculty for over one hundred years. I rested against my tote bag that I had placed near me on the bench and perused a novel I had been reading when I found spare time until Grayson appeared blowing his horn to indicate it was time to leave.

"Sorry I'm late, sweetie," he said, as he came around and ushered me into the passenger side of the car. "My last clients were late and it threw me behind just a little."

"Oh, that's okay. It's so beautiful outside today. I can't complain about anything." I smiled and allowed my head to fall back on the headrest.

Grayson steered the car with ease out of the parking lot. He smiled at me as I wriggled down and reclined the seat to get comfortable.

We exchanged pleasantries and spoke about the events of the

day until there was a quiet lull in the conversation. Buildings and cars glided past us as we drove away from town. I found the drive soothing while I surrendered to the tranquil expressions of the jazz CD that was playing.

Rush hour was always maddening, and Grayson usually took the back roads that lead away from the hectic downtown traffic. There was hardly a car in sight on the back streets, and I sighed in sheer delight of the afternoon. The houses gave the illusion of a fairyland that seemed to convey peace and serenity from those homes that were sometimes hidden by the lush foliage of the summer season behind quaint gates. I closed my eyes and allowed the music, which summoned peaceful musings to my mind, to wash over me as we drove until Grayson finally parked the car. My eyes slid open, and I observed that we were outside his apartment building.

"I thought you said that we were going to have dinner?" I asked.

"We are," he said and hopped out of the car with a grin. "My lady." He extended his hand to help me from the vehicle.

I smiled and shook my head at him in amusement, wondering at his whimsical behavior as we rode the elevator to the third floor. I knew that he had not relinquished the idea of my moving in with him, so I mentally braced myself for the onslaught of questions later.

It was cool in his apartment, and the blinds had been drawn against the afternoon sun. He guided me to the sofa, pressed a button on a remote, and similar strains of music that had played in the car now flowed through the living room. He disappeared into the kitchen and quickly returned with a glass of sweet iced tea which he handed me.

"This is for you." I looked up, and he was now offering me a beautiful long stemmed red rose that he had concealed behind his back.

"Oh, Gray," I smiled and released a soft giggle. "You're so sweet."

"Why don't you just stretch out on the sofa?" he came around, removed my shoes and placed my feet on the couch, gave me a kiss on the cheek, and headed for the kitchen. "I'll get things together for dinner."

I did as I was instructed, snuggling down into the confines of the sofa, occasionally sipping the sweet amber liquid, and flipped through a magazine that I had picked up from his coffee table.

"Something smells good," I called over my shoulder.

"I hope you'll like it," he answered from somewhere in the kitchen.

I let my mind drift on the melodious road of dissonant chords that danced through the cool, dim room. I rested my head on one of the pillows that flanked the sofa. I placed the tea on top of the magazine I had placed back on the table and sighed as the music swept me away to some distant, mystical, place that was serene and beautiful.

My eyelids fluttered until my dark lashes finally rested, and there was a lull between the conscious and subconscious. The music carried me into a dense mist. Further and further into the mist I went until the dream of the Huntsman filled my mind. It was the same dream. Only I was running now, searching, for who or what I did not know. I stopped and turned, and the dream shifted as dreams often do.

Before I Wake

I saw someone in the distance, but it wasn't the Huntsman. I could only see the silhouette of a woman that appeared to shift in and out of the mist. She moved as if she folded in and out of the space. She was there but not there. Not in but not out. I started running toward her, but the more I ran, the further away the figure seemed to be from me. Finally, I stopped. My senses were keenly aware of the woman's presence. More than actually seeing her, I suddenly felt her presence in the smoky haze. I reached out a hand toward the figure.

"Mama?" I said. "Mama, is that you?" I walked toward the figure, and I could feel her gently touching my shoulder. "Mama, Mama..."

"Souline, honey," I heard my name through the fog. The voice was familiar but confusing. It wasn't my mother. "Souline baby, wake up." I felt a hand gently shaking my shoulder to rouse me from sleep. The images dissipated like the shimmering, fragile, color of a butterfly's wing that erases under the most delicate of touches.

"It's time for dinner." I heard the very male voice of Grayson speaking to me. He watched as my very heavy lids fluttered slowly, and then opened. "You were calling your mother."

"I was?" I asked as remnants of the dream begin to dispel.

"Are you okay?" He asked concern evident on his face. "Were you dreaming about her?"

I nodded and shrugged my shoulder. "I suppose. It's rather fragmented now." He smiled as I sat up and released a delicate yawn that I stifled with the back of my hand. I stood, stretched and he allowed an appreciative gaze to follow me as I walked from the room to wash up for dinner.

After dinner, we retired to the sofa. Conversation during dinner had been as inviting as the meal that he had prepared. We had a green salad, baked chicken, mashed potatoes, glazed carrots and there had also been a light sorbet for dessert.

I rested my head on his chest and sighed as we listened to a new jazz selection that had automatically changed while we chatted. I could hear his heart beat and his slow, steady, breath as I lay there unmoving and content.

"Souline?" The rumble of his voice made me feel warm inside.

I had sighed, just a little before I said, "Humm?"

"Did you think about what I asked you the other day?"

"What other day, Gray?" I offered languidly through another sigh that was given in delicious comfort.

"What I asked the other day about us being together," he reminded me.

My head shot up from his chest, and I blinked.

"Oh!" The surprise was evident in my voice, and I stiffened. I was annoyed with myself for letting my guard down when I had promised so faithfully that I would not allow that to happen.

"Gray..." I hedged.

"Yes, sweetheart," he said, with a warm patience that for some reason I found annoying.

"I thought you were going to let this drop?" I lied. I knew that he was going to bring the subject up again. I was hoping that it would not have been so soon.

"How could I just let it drop? Besides, you're always complaining about the situation with your family, and this isn't the first time this has come up either. You've told me that you wanted a different life. So I'm offering you a life, with me."

"Gray, it's not that simple." I was stalling. I kept thinking that a flash of inspiration would hit me, or maybe a bolt of lightning would just hit me so that I would not have to have this conversation at all.

"Why not? It's only as complicated as you make it," he said evenly, unwilling to let the conversation drop, but being careful not to make me anymore defensive.

"Well, for one thing, my financial situation won't allow me to share an apartment with you. Winn and I share the expenses at home, plus the provisions Granddaddy Joe left for Gran. As it is, I'm barely able to put a little money aside for my dance studio. You know that I've always dreamed of having my own dance studio and making it into a viable business. I know that it's going to take time and money." I said hoping that this would deter him. I also knew that I was using this as an excuse to wiggle out of the conversation. I was desperately grasping at straws, not quite sure what I should say.

"I never asked you to pay rent," he said flatly.

"I never expected to live anywhere without paying my share." I lifted my chin defiantly.

"Souline..." he said carefully. "Do you know why I sell real estate?" His gaze was unswerving.

I looked at him and shook my head unsure where this line of questioning was leading.

"Because," he continued. "I enjoy it. And, do you know why I enjoy it?" I shook my head again slowly, and he continued. "Not to brag or anything, but I enjoy it because I'm good at it. Money is the least of your concerns. I am a good provider, and I want you here with me because I love you and because I want to take care of you. I've always loved you, and I think you know that. I want to share my life with you."

I looked at him as said, "Gray...I don't want to live with you."

He looked stunned and crestfallen, and I quickly amended the statement. "What I mean is..." I scrambled to correct the overly direct comment I had made because I saw the hurt in his eyes. "I don't want to just live with any man. I don't want to be any man's live-in partner. I grew up understanding that if I'm good enough to share your life, your home, and your bed, then I should be good enough to share your name. I'm just not the mistress type, Gray."

He looked at me slightly bewildered.

"You are all that I want in the world," he said. "You are all that make sense to me. You are the person that possesses a place in my heart that no other woman ever can or will. You are that part of my being that makes me breathe, that part of my spirit that makes me feel alive. I'm not asking you to move in with me."

I blinked somewhat confused, "Then I don't understand." I said.

"I'm asking you to marry me," he stated simply.

There was a sharp intake of breath, as my hand flew to my mouth. There it was! He had said it. It was out there, and it could be taken back.

"Grayson..." I said, somewhat dumbfounded, even though I knew that he was going to ask. I knew that he cared for me and cared deeply, but I did not think that he would seriously pursue the topic of marriage. Or maybe I did. I just hoped that he would not have pursued the idea right now at this time in our lives. "I-I..." was all I could manage.

"Honey, I never wanted you just to move in with me. You must have known that, Souline? I love you. And I know that it's a little old-fashioned, but if a man really loves a woman, he would never place her in a position where she is not honored by other men. She is never really protected as his mistress. I would never hurt you that way. I would never ask you to live a lie."

"Grayson..."

He placed both his hands on my shoulders and gently turned me toward him so that I could see just how earnest those calm dark brown eyes were, and he asked, "Do you know the reason I call you Soul? It's not just because it's a nickname, but because that's what you are to me, Souline. You are my... my soul. You make me whole, and I want to share everything with you. You're my heartbeat, Souline. I know that I didn't really ask you properly the other day, but I'm asking you now."

He looked at me with a sincerity that moved something undetectable within me, and he asked again, "Souline, will you marry me?" Just as he asked, he reached behind him and pulled out a beautiful little navy blue velvet box and showed it to me.

"Grayson," I whispered, more than just a little overwhelmed and unsure as to how I should start.

"You will never need or want for anything. If it is within my power, I will make sure you have it," he said sincerely.

"Gray, I honestly did not expect you to ask me to marry you. I mean, not right now. We're both still fairly young. I thought you might want to do things with your life."

"I do," he said with longing in his eyes. "I just want to do them with you."

"I don't know what to say." I desperately tried to find an answer that would appease him. I knew that he cared for me, and I cared for him too. We had been friends since we were children. I just never dreamed that he would go as far as to actually ask me to marry him. I always thought that I would be able to tell him just what I felt no matter what the circumstance, but right now, at this moment I was honestly at a loss for words.

"Say yes," he said.

I looked at him with sympathy, but I said, "I can't, Gray." I placed my hand over his hand that held the little box and pushed his fingers around it as if to urge him to put it away.

Those dark brown eyes clouded over with some ineffable emotion for a split second and then vanished. They searched mine for something that would help him to understand my hesitation but was unable to discern my reasoning. I did not want to hurt him, but I did not want to lie to him either.

"You can't or you won't, Souline," he said, the hurt in his eyes was reflected in his voice. He looked at me as if I had thrust a spear into his heart and he was trying to make sense of my action.

"I'm just not ready to marry that's all," I said touching his arm gently. "I want to see the world. I want to see and do new things. Can you understand that?"

"Yes," He spoke quietly. "I can understand that. I just thought that we could see the world together. We could plan a lifetime together."

"Gray, please..." I said, not wanting to pursue the painful topic any longer. He threw up his hands, not angry, but obviously not happy either.

"I'll tell you what," he said. "You're not saying that you don't want to get married. You're just saying that you don't want to marry, now. Right? Well, we don't have to decide right at this moment. Why don't we just let it rest for now? Okay?"

"Okay," I agreed a little too quickly, desperately wanting to get out of this situation. I knew that I should have objected to his suggestion, but something inside of me that I could not quite identify stopped me.

We allowed the subject to drop.

The drive home was quiet, we said very little to each other. He was not angry, but he was lost in thought, and I let him stay there. To keep my mind occupied, I watched the poles that lined the streets pass like giant sentinels illuminating the road with intermittent splashes of light. The dull yellow glow was a reminder to the darkness that it was its master.

When we reached home, Grayson walked me to the front door, lightly kissed me goodnight on the cheek, and said that he would see me in the morning. I nodded, let myself in the house, and allowed a long slow breath to escape from my breast as I slumped against the front door and closed out all of the concerns of a long, strenuous day.

CHAPTER ELEVEN

And the angel said unto her.

Luke 1:30(KJV)

6:28 a.m. Wednesday, June 12, 20__

"If you are just tuning in, millions of residents in the Pacific Northwest are facing the worst natural disaster in U.S. history since Hurricane Katrina. On Tuesday evening at 5:57 p.m. PDT, a magnitude nine earthquake struck what is known as the Cascadia Subduction Zone, causing an unprecedented series of deadly waves that have left the Pacific coastline devastated.

The quake's deadly force unleashed a series of tsunamis where coastal communities have been hit hard by waves that have reached up to sixty feet in height. Waves were clocked at top speeds of an estimated 450 mph, causing landslides and leaving coastal areas devastated and inundated with water.

Tsunami warnings were also issued for the coastal areas of Japan where twenty-foot waves were reported to have struck the country's eastern coastlines. The initial quake lasted for about ten minutes, and so far 50,000 people are reported dead or missing, and millions are homeless, from as far north as the Coastal Range of British Columbia, to as far south as California. The death toll is expected to go higher.

And now a look other world news, arrangements are being made to ship the remains of world leader, Hadrian Maxmillian, back to his homeland, where funeral arrangements will be made later this week. Mr. Maxmillian, who initiated The New World Peace Treaty, was allegedly attacked by known terrorist, Omar Mohammad while entering his car after leaving the Global Summit. The world leader was pronounced dead at the scene Monday evening; he had sustained a fatal wound to the head after his alleged assailant slipped past his bodyguards and stabbed him. Other sources report..."

I had not slept well and had gotten up late. My dreams had been filled with a mass of tangled images where the Huntsman and Grayson had been chasing me. In the dream, I was wearing a full-length wedding gown, running and Grayson was trying to catch me. He kept calling my name over and over.

I woke to the voice of Gran calling me from somewhere downstairs telling me that I was going to be late for work. I answered in some unintelligible language and dragged my body out of bed to prepare for school.

After showering and dressing, I yawned and padded down the steps into the living room where Winn and Gran watched the news reports intently.

"This is just unbelievable," Winn said, horrified by the devastation that was displayed on the television screen.

"What's unbelievable?" I asked, and yawned a second time,

stopping behind my grandmother's wheelchair and kissing the top of her head, and then hugging Winn, who sat on the sofa watching the dreadful news report. Winn gave me a brief account of the tsunami report and it quickly registered on my brain.

"Oh, my goodness, how awful!" I exclaimed expressing my disbelief. My eyes grew wider with interest as I stared at the television.

"It's just the times we're living in," Gran said. "It's getting worse day by day."

"I know," Winn responded, awestruck and nodding in agreement.

"This is just what we were telling Grayson the other day. I believe that we are the generation that is witnessing the fulfillment of prophecies of the last days," Gran said.

I didn't say anything. I was not in the mood to hear her expound on prophetic disasters of biblical proportion.

"Well, I'd better get some breakfast. Grayson's going to be here any moment," I said, by way of excusing myself and hurried to leave the room.

I walked into the well-organized kitchen and grabbed the scrambled eggs and a couple of pieces of bacon that were left on a plate on top of the stove. I stood over the pristine kitchen sink snatching bites of the lopsided sandwich I had made because I knew that I didn't have time to sit and eat breakfast. I took two gulps of the coffee I had poured when I realized that I had not brought down my tote bag for today's classes.

With part of the sandwich still in my mouth, nearly crashing into my grandmother who was entering the kitchen, I made a dash up the steps towards my bedroom, taking two steps at a time. I grabbed the bag from my bed and hoped that I might have another cup of coffee before Grayson arrived. As I hurried from my room toward the landing, I saw Winn standing just outside of her bedroom in the hallway.

"You're going to be late for work standing there daydreaming," I said, and smiled at her and proceeded toward the staircase.

Winn did not respond.

Instead, she stood there as if she was frozen in time.

"Winn?" I glanced at her and gave a little chuckle, and when she did not respond, this time, I stopped on the stairs and stared back at her. "Winn?" I called again. My brows furrowed, and I noticed that Winn did not seem to even be aware of my presence. I turned on the stair. Winn never moved from that statue-like position that she held, and it made the hairs stand up on my arms. I walked back up the stairs and inched slowly toward my sister. I stopped near her and started to put my hand out to touch her, but I hesitated, not quite sure what I should do next.

"Winn?" I spoke softly. Her eyes were fixed on a single point, and she moved her mouth as if she was carrying on a conversation with someone. Only there was no sound emanating from her, and there certainly was no one standing there in front of her. A shiver ran through me.

"Winn..." I said this time alarmed by her behavior. I passed a hand before her face several times to see if I could break the trance she seemed to have slipped into. "Winn!" I raised a frightened voice and shook her non-too-gently. Winn snapped out of her dazed state. Her head drooped backward, and I grabbed her by the arms to keep her from falling. She shook her head with some lethargy as she moved out of the trance. She seemed to have some difficulty focusing, and looked at me as if she was returning from some place far away.

"Are you alright?" I asked, half frightened and half relieved from the anxiety that I had felt. "What were you doing? I asked, taking her by the arm and leading her to her bedroom. "Here, come and lie down for a moment."

"Oh, I'm..." Winn said, and nearly fainted as her head sagged backward. I grabbed her around the waist and guided her toward the bed. Winn walked as if she was in a drunken stupor. I helped her to sit down on the bed and rushed into her bathroom to retrieve a cool washcloth and press it against her face and forehead.

"Put your head between your knees." Winn did as she was told for a few minutes and then finally raised her head slowly and shook it again as if she was still trying to focus.

"What were you doing?" I asked again. "You were standing there as if you were carrying on a conversation with someone.

Winn cast a furtive glance at me while she was still trying to gain her composure. She looked as if she was debating whether she should tell me what she was doing or not.

"I-I was..." She started with some hesitation. "You won't believe me if I tell you," she said and regarded me speculatively.

"Of course I will," I said and patted her hand, trying to assure her and coax her at the same time.

She looked at me from under her lashes and said, "I-I was talking..." she hesitated once again and took a deep breath as if she was summoning every ounce of courage she possessed.

"You were talking...Yes—go on, Sweetie," I prompted, fearing that she may require some medical attention.

She spoke in hushed tones as if someone was eavesdropping. "I was talking, t-to an angel," she finally said and watched me as if she was searching for a reassuring response.

I chuckled nervously for a second and then my breath caught in my throat. I stared at Winn as if she had two heads which would have been easier for me to accept for some reason.

"Winn, that's not funny," I said flatly. "You almost fainted again." I had lost my patience with her and said peevishly, "I'm standing here wondering if you need to go to a doctor, and you're kidding about something that could potentially be a serious medical condition. I am half frightened to death about all of the fainting spells that you've been having, and you're making jokes at a time like this?"

"I'm not joking, Souline. I was talking to an angel," she insisted and looked down at her hands, disappointed that I had not believed her.

I gave her a blank stare. I didn't quite know what to say. I searched her face half expecting a grin to appear and for Winn to reveal her rather impish sense of humor. But, deep down, I knew that Winn, nor my grandmother, would ever joke about anything so in line with the framework of their faith. There was a rapt expression that had settled on my sister's features. There was something that I could not quite put my finger on that seemed to emanate from the inside of her, something that seemed rather otherworldly, and I found it disturbing. There was also an undeniable sincerity in all that she said. Not that

Winn was a liar, far from it, as a matter of fact, most of the time she could be brutally honest when dealing with others, especially when it came to her faith. But, for the life of me, I just could not let myself accept such an incredible notion.

However, it was obvious that she had experienced something, but at the moment I could not say exactly what it was.

"Winn, what are you saying? Are you trying to tell me that you were carrying on a conversation...?"

"I'm not *trying* to tell you anything..." she interrupted, "I'm telling you that I spoke with an angel!"

The statement was quiet but emphatic, and I found myself at a loss for words. Just at that moment, Gran called up the stairs to tell me that Grayson was waiting outside.

"I'm going to tell Grayson that I'm not going in today, and you're going to the doctor," I said, recovering my voice as I walked toward the door, concerned about both her physical and mental well-being.

"Why?" she protested. "I'm not staying at home. I'm going to work."

"No, you're not," I was adamant.

"I'm alright, don't start fussing over me," she said annoyed.

"Winn, I'm not fussing. I just don't think that it's wise for you to go to work today. You need to go to the doctor, or at the very least you need to stay home and rest. You've been working too hard." I offered as an excuse to explain the theory of her heavenly encounter. I was not ready to give into the idea of my sister carrying on a conversation with a celestial being.

""I'm fine," she said and waved me away.

"Winn, this isn't something you can just toss away. You're going to the doctor and that's final," I said determinedly.

"No, I'm not," she said peevishly. I'm going to work." She was just as determined.

"Winn...," I started, but Winn got up and gently pushed me toward the door.

"Souline?" Gran called again. "Grayson's waiting, Baby."

"Go! I'll be alright, and we'll talk later. You're going to be late for work. Don't keep that man waiting." The mischievous twinkle had returned to her eyes.

"Winn..." I hesitated.

"I'm okay, but I want to talk to you when you get home this afternoon. Okay?"

"I...Oooh, Okay!" I sighed in exasperation and gave in. I hugged her and ran downstairs. I was frustrated because I knew that for all of my insisting, she was not going to do as I had asked. I thought maybe Gran might be able to persuade her to go to the doctor if I could not.

I gave a brief account of the occurrence to my grandmother. I had not wanted to go into detail about Winn's encounter with a heavenly host, but I implored her to make Winn stay home from work and get some rest if she could not make her go to the doctor. Gran assured me that she would talk to Winn, and told me not to worry about her.

When I got into the car, my mind was honed on a single point for most of the morning commute. To say that I was distracted would have been an understatement. An angel of all things for goodness sake, what on earth was that all about? I desperately wanted to discount the entire incident and pretend that nothing had happened.

However, when I remembered Winn's face while she was carrying on that unspoken conversation, I could not dismiss the incident so easily. I was forced to admit that Winn looked almost otherworldly as she just stood there, with a euphoric expression on her face. I did not want to think that Winn had actually had some supernatural encounter. That would mean that I would have to admit that Winn might have been communicating with a being from another realm, which was just too much for me to accept at the moment.

So what exactly had happened? Had I been witnessing the beginning of the degeneration of my sister's mental faculties? Was this behavior related to the fainting spells she has been experiencing? If she was having some sort of mental collapse, what could I do to help her? I shivered inwardly.

"And I thought that I'd drive straight across the Atlantic Ocean to London, non-stop, not even for gas. What do you think?"

Bits and pieces of a voice etched into my thoughts and registered as Grayson spoke to me, and I tried to shake off the unsettling events of the morning.

"What?" I said, as my mind caught snatches of his conversation trying to bring me back to the present.

"Earth to Souline," he said, concerned about the uneasy expression that had settled on my face. "You don't have to worry. I'm not going to bring up last night's topic again." He took my hand in his and kissed it.

"Oh, that's not what I was thinking about," I said absently.

"Gee thanks," he drawled sardonically and then offered a slight smile. "What's got you so thoughtful this morning—family troubles?" He asked, and winced when he realized what he had said. "Sorry, I didn't mean it that way, I mean I..."

I ignored the comment, smiled, and waved it away. I kept my eyes on the road in front of me. I did not want to tell him what had happened with Winn. How do you tell someone, even your best friend, that your sister just had a conversation with an angel? I had not even been able to bring myself to voice the occurrence to my grandmother. So how on earth could I explain something so incredulous to him when I could not accept such a notion myself?

"No, I just have a lot on my mind this morning, that's all," I said.

"Anything you want to share," he asked sincerely. "I've got two ears, no waiting," he smiled.

"No," I smiled and touched his hand. "Thanks."

"Okay," he said and smiled. A silence fell between us once again.

The car consumed the last few miles of our journey, and he let me out in front of the school. We both said our goodbyes, and with the promise of his afternoon's return and ride home, he drove away.

The day was particularly trying. I was distracted during the morning routine. I obviously had quite a lot on my mind. The suspicion that my sister could very well be having a mental meltdown coupled with the fact that Grayson had asked me to marry him, left me feeling emotionally disheveled. I felt as though there were bits and pieces of me that were scattered about, and I didn't know where to start to pick up the tattered pieces. And lately, for some inexplicable reason, the death of my mother was uppermost on my mind. There was also an undercurrent of expectancy that I could not shake, and it was making me feel uneasy; an inexplicable feeling that lingered in the back of my mind as if something was about to happen.

What on earth is the matter with me? Maybe I'm a little on edge because I had not slept well over the past few nights. However, when I do sleep my dreams are so unsettling that they disturb my peace. Why do I keep dreaming about the Huntsman? I haven't had that dream in ages.

I relinquished my line of thought and tried to concentrate on the tasks that lay before me. I called Gran to see if Winn was feeling better, only to be informed that Winn brushed aside the incident and decided to go to work. Try as I might to concentrate, the daily routine of each class performance was a blur. At intervals, thoughts of Winn and Grayson interrupted my teaching duties. The only thing I recalled was the last bell that informed me that the school day had come to an end.

I walked in front of the mirrors that lined the studio walls and stood *en pointe*. I performed a few routines of pointe work and decided that I had better gather my belongings so that Grayson would not have to wait.

CHAPTER TWELVE

Even so thou knowest not the works of God who maketh all.

Ecclesiastes 11:5 (KJV)

3:07 p.m. Wednesday, June 12, 20__

Grayson was waiting in the car when I walked outside. I reached the car door and sat down in my seat before he had time to get out and usher me into the vehicle.

"Sorry, I'm late," I said, my voice sounding strained to my ears, as I stared absently out of the window. "You're not late, Honey," he said and smiled.

"Gray," I said, turning toward him. "Can we go somewhere please? I mean, are you in a hurry to get home?" I silently pleaded with some unknown force that he would not want to go home right at this moment.

"No, not really," he said, uneasiness settled behind his usually placid eyes. "What's wrong, baby? You looked tired." His brow furrowed when he noticed the strain that was evident on my face. He caressed my cheek with his finger and maneuvered the car onto the road with his free hand.

"Oh nothing," I said with a sigh.

"And everything?" He gave an impudent wink and smiled at me. I relinquished a weak smile at his wink and leaned my head against the headrest.

"I'm just not ready to go home right now, that's all." My mind was like a pot that was filled to the brim and to the point of boiling over. I just needed time to allow the flame to die down and let things simmer.

"Why don't we grab something to eat and go to the park?" he asked. I nodded gratefully and said, "Thanks."

We stopped by *Mr. Chow's Chinese Emporium*, to pick up an assortment of Chinese take-out dishes, and drove toward the river park. Grayson parked the car and grabbed the blanket he always kept in his trunk. Together we went in search of a spot to sit, eat, and reflect. The river ran through the huge mass of land that was Summerville's major park area. The grass was a rich emerald green that had been well cared for and cultivated.

We spread the blanket near a great weeping willow tree that overlooked the river. Grayson placed the bag with the food in it on the blanket and turned to helped me to settle comfortably. The earth felt like a soft downy mattress beneath us, and we watched in silence for a while, as the bright sparkles of the warm amber sun danced on the river that sauntered past us while we ate.

There was a huge barge on the water that lazily inched past

some of the most elite of Summerville's dwellings that rested on the southern shore of the river. Grayson, breaking the silence, told me a number of interesting facts about many of the homes lining the shore, including the cost, for which I listened, coughed and blinked in disbelief at the exorbitant price of one beautiful, gray, stone house that was directly in my view.

"Good, grief!" I exclaimed as my jaw dropped. "I knew that they were expensive, but I had no idea they cost that much."

"Yep," he said, laughing at the astonished look on my face. "But you should see the inside of some of them, Soul. You would love them. Maybe one day, I might be able to afford a home for... uh, I mean." He had stopped himself before he included me in his future plans for a home. "Sorry," he said, sheepishly and gnashed his teeth, casting his eyes upward to escape the empathetic look I gave him.

"Don't be sorry, Gray," I said, not without compassion. "Someday maybe, but just not right now, okay?" He cast a wane smile my way and dropped his gaze toward a piece of beef that he moved around in his container.

He turned on his back and placed a hand underneath his head. He stared through the dark green foliage and found patches of blue sky that darted through the leaves. He felt a little more hopeful than he had before. At least it was not an emphatic no, he thought; as he turned a furtive eye toward her to steal a glimpse at her. She was the loveliest woman he had ever known. Not that there was a long line of females knocking down his door, but he had never lacked female companionship. There had been a few women that had caught his eye along the way, but his heart's compass had always brought him back to Souline. His mind skipped back to a place in his heart where he stored his fondest memories of her. He remembered helping her with homework and showing her how to keep her balance when he taught her to skate. He even remembered helping to patch up those skinny knees with Band-Aids on more than one occasion. There was also the time he had taught her to drive his motorcycle. She had sent three of the neighbors' trash bins flying, and came to a screeching halt just before she totally annihilated Mrs. Jackson's entire rose garden. He smiled, when he remembered their youthful antics and gave a small sigh as he allowed his eyes to tenderly caress her lithe figure. Were these legs that curled so gracefully underneath her now, the same ones that he helped to patch up and bandage in their youth? That seemed a lifetime ago. He smiled.

"What are you smiling about?" I asked. I had been observing him while he was lost in thought and fought an impulse to kiss him.

"Oh, I was just thinking about yesterday."

"What about yesterday?" I asked puzzled.

"Never mind," he gave and enigmatic smile at the reference and changed the subject. "Why didn't you want to go home?" he asked as he turned on his stomach and stirred the noodles around in the carryout carton.

"I-I don't know," I hesitated. The rush of memory concerning Winn flooded my mind, and my brows snapped together with anxiety.

"I'm sorry. I didn't mean to pry." He stabbed at a wonton noodle with his chopstick, when he observed my face and my evasive manner.

"You're not prying. I'm just not sure how to tell you this," I said, with my gaze fixed on the carryout container that I held.

"What's wrong now?" he asked gently. His steady gaze searched my face as if he was trying to unravel some clue as to what was causing my hesitation. "Did you have another argument with your family?" He asked in earnest without any interest for his concerns.

"No, nothing like that," I answered, moving a piece of chicken around in the carton as if it would help to divine a way of explaining my sister's behavior. He patiently waited for me to gather my thoughts. I looked at him, took a deep breath and summoned my courage.

"This morning..." I hesitated. "This morning before you came to pick me up when I came out of my bedroom. I-I saw Winn standing in the hallway...talking..." I managed to stumble out.

He looked perplexed, "Talking?" he questioned. He realized that there was more than I was telling him since I was obviously struggling with the explanation. He asked in a coaxing manner, "What's wrong with talking?"

"Well, not exactly talking, more like..." I searched my mind for the correct phrase, but words failed me. "She was sorta... Oh, I don't know how to explain it. It was more like pantomiming than actually talking to someone." He cocked his head to the side and gave me a quizzical look as if he was waiting for me to reveal the punch line to a joke.

"I'm sorry, I'm not following," he said, with a polite shake of his head.

"Gray, she was talking, but there was no sound and there was no one there." I blurted out. "It was as if she was in a stupor or something, I don't know, I can't explain it." I placed my head in my hands to try and gather my thoughts. "Anyway," I said and lifted my head. "When she came out of it, and I asked her what she was doing," I took another deep breath before I continued. "She said that she had been talking to... to an angel."

His head shot up from the container, and his hand stopped in mid-air just as he was about to bite into a noodle. He blinked at me, gave a little nervous chuckle, and looked at me as if he was not sure if he had heard me correctly. At first, he thought that I was joking, but when he saw my face, he knew that I was serious. He stared at me and let out a long, low, whistle.

"Are you serious?" he asked, out of sheer disbelief.

"Yes. I'm serious! Who would make up something like that?"

"I know, but you know, Winn, she does have a rather quirky sense of humor. Are you sure that she wasn't just pulling your leg?"

"No, Gray, she was dead serious, and if you had seen the look on her face, it would have made the hairs stand up on the back of your neck. It was as if she was in some kind of trance, and when she came out of it, she tried to dismiss the incident. But, so help me, Gray, it scared the heck out of me."

He put down the cardboard container he was eating from, and pulled me to him, and I let my head rest on his shoulder. "Is there anything that I can do to help?" He asked sincerely.

"No, nothing that I can think of," I said. "It was just so weird seeing her that way. Standing there carrying on a conversation with the air."

"Do you think that she may need some kind of counseling?" He asked tentatively, trying not to add to my anxiety.

"I don't know. That's what's so disturbing about all of this. She looked so sincere when she told me about the angel. She said that she wanted to talk to me later this evening. Maybe after we talk, I can try and figure out what's going on with her.

If it's any consolation, being here with you this afternoon has meant more to me that you'll ever know," I said and reached up and kissed him softly on the cheek.

"I'm always here for you," he said. "You know that?"

A slight nod was the silent answer I gave him.

He hugged me, and we sat in the peaceful surroundings of the park for some time, watching the sleepy river roll by, people passing, birds flying overhead, and the occasional boat darting across the water. We stayed there and talked until dusk painted the sky with huge splashes of mauve, yellow and orange and the sunlight began to fade as it began to lower itself behind the horizon. Finally, we picked up our containers, folded our blanket, and headed for home.

CHAPTER THIRTEEN

Your dream and the visions that passed through your mind as you lay on your bed
are these.

Daniel 2:28 (NIV)

7:17 p.m.-Thursday, June 13, 20___

"I'm going to the kitchen, anybody want anything while I'm up?" I asked, as Winn and Gran sat in the living room and talked about the upcoming youth concert. I had been sitting on the sofa, absently thumbing through a dated magazine. I wasn't really interested in hearing the latest updates concerning Pastor Martin and the members of Pleasant View Baptist Church. My workday had been uneventful and I was enjoying the treasured freedom of sitting at home in peace.

They each answered no to my question and continued their conversation while I went into the kitchen and sliced a piece of chocolate cake that I knew I did not need. I decided to indulge in my cake outside on the front porch where I could get some fresh air. About fifteen minutes later, Gran and Winn joined me.

For a good part of the evening, we sat on the front porch and talked. I sat quietly as they finished their conversation about church business. I closed my eyes and let my head rest against the porch swing as I gently rocked back and forth. The heat of the day had waned and finally settled into a pleasant summer night. The soft, bulbous, blooms of the street lamps cast a hazy glow along the quiet road that was occasionally interrupted by a neighbor finally making his or her way home.

The sound of a dog barking in some obscure distance floated on the savory breeze that rustled the leaves of plants and trees, which were sporadically lit by a multitude of fireflies that flashed like hundreds of Christmas lights in the lush foliage.

I continued to rock the porch swing that I shared with my sister, back and forth with my foot, slowly and methodically. The gentle squeak of the swing seemed to blend with the songs of the chirping crickets and add an air of tranquility to the quiet moment that had fallen between us.

I sighed, hating to break the peace that had settled within the circle of the three of us as we took in the evening air. But I said, "Gray asked me to marry him," the words floated from me in the soft darkness of the night.

"Oooo!" A tiny shriek of excitement escaped from Winn as she clapped her hands. "It's about time." I could see her smile in the dim lighting as she reached to hug me. "I knew that he would get around to it eventually. When did he ask you?"

"Tuesday," I said simply.

"And you're just telling us? Some sister you are," she chuckled. "Come toward the front door, near the light so I can see the ring." Winn jumped to her feet heading toward the door, pulling at my left arm.

"There is no ring," I said dryly.

"What?" Winn allowed my arm to gently fall from her grasp, shock evident in her voice.

"There is no ring," Gran repeated.

"And why not?" Winn seemed more than just a little peeved. "That boy doesn't strike me as being cheap! I know that he's quite capable of buying you a decent engagement ring. Is he waiting for some special moment to spring it on you?"

"No. He offered a ring. I didn't accept his proposal," I said evenly.

"Oh, Souline, why not?" She whined, unable to hide her disappointment. "How could you do such a thing? He is so in love with you!"

"Because I'm not ready, Winn," I said, rather defensively.

"But he's a good man! What do you need to do to be ready, for heaven's sake?" She said, with some annoyance.

"Well now, Winn," Gran offered, "You have to let people go along at their own pace, honey."

I was a little-taken aback by her comment. I had thought for sure that she would have sided with Winn and Gray on this matter.

"If she goes any slower, he's gonna find someone else."

"Well if that's the case then he doesn't deserve a granddaughter of mine," Gran stated emphatically, her chin jutting out proudly. "Although I don't think that he will," she said with a chuckle.

I blinked in disbelief. I knew that my grandmother was very fond of Grayson, and I knew that she hoped that we would get married. I was very surprised that she was defending my position on the subject.

"I think that if you just give her time to sort things out you might eventually be an aunt. Ain't that right, baby?" She said, and reached across her wheelchair to pat my hand.

"Thanks, Gran," I rubbed her hand against my cheek, grateful for her support. I drew my knees underneath me in the swing.

"Well, I think that she should say yes to the man, and get on with her life."

"Well, that's just the point," I snapped at her just a bit more forcefully than I intended. "It's *my* life isn't it? I just want to do a few things with it before I settle down."

"What kind of things?" Winn asked slightly exasperated with me.

"I want to see some of the world. I want to travel, maybe have my own school for dancing. I don't know, but like Gran said, I want time to figure things out. And I'm not going to be pressured into a situation, I'm not ready to handle. If I did that, all I'd wind up doing is making Gray and me very unhappy. Whether you believe me or not, I care enough about him not to make his life miserable," I said testily.

"Humph!" was Winn's irritated reply, and she shot a

disapproving glance my way that spoke volumes, but it went unobserved in the evening shadows. She was a little frustrated with me. However, she did not voice her opinion and allowed the conversation to lapse. She changed the direction of the discussion by commenting on repairs that needed to be made on the house, and the conversation eventually subsided.

It was a short time later, before Gran finally said, "Well girls, this old woman's got to get her beauty sleep," and chuckled to herself.

"Yes, we need to go in as well. It's past ten, and we're not going to be fit for anything in the morning," I said, as both Winn and I rose to our feet. I held the door open, and Gran wheeled herself up the small ramp and into the living room.

"I want to water my plants before I go to bed. I'll check both doors and turned out the downstairs lights when I'm done."

Gran grabbed the remote, flipped on the television, and wheeled herself around the living room, bent on the mission of watering her potted plant family. She was talking to them, and telling some of the little green things that were not flourishing in the way that she wanted them to; and that she may have to move their homes to another part of the house where they could grow and be happy.

She was talking to a Wandering Jew, which she had named Moses, saying that he was outgrowing his home, when she abruptly paused and cocked her head to one side, focusing her attention on a news report coming from the television.

Winn and I were headed upstairs when we heard the crash of pottery near Gran.

Before I Wake

"Gran...," we said in unison. Running downstairs to see if she needed help.

"What's wrong? I asked and looked to see what she had broken. Do you...?"

"Shhhh," I was effectively silenced, with an abrupt wave of her hand. She hurriedly wheeled herself around toward the television and abruptly stopped in front of the set. "Listen!" she demanded.

Winn and I glanced at each other and then turned toward the screen trying to see what had grabbed our Grandmother's attention.

A smartly dressed female reporter sitting behind the news desk was saying, "If you're just tuning in, the global community is stunned by the extraordinary recovery of world leader Hadrian Maxmillian. Doctors are saying his recovery is an unprecedented miracle. Mr. Maxmillian, after attending the World Summit, received a fatal wound to the head Monday while entering his car, by known terrorist, Omar Mohammad. Mr. Maxmillian was pronounced dead at the scene Monday evening around 6:00 p.m. EST. However, this morning just after midnight, he was found wandering the halls after his remains had been placed in the hospital morgue. The remains were to be shipped today to his homeland to be interred. Doctors are expected to give an update on Mr. Maxmillian's condition at a news conference that will be held tomorrow morning at St. Andrew Hospital, where he is being held for further observation. Once again, world leader, Hadrian Maximillian..."

Gran and Winn both cast a knowing glance at each other, as if they were privy to some secret information that I was not.

"He has got to be the one," Gran said with quiet conviction.

"I think so too, Gran," Winn said with an unsettling chill in her voice. I glanced surreptitiously from one and then to the other, wondering what could they possibly be talking about with such chilling undertones.

"You know, just the other day Ida and I both said that we've had such an uneasy feeling in our spirits about this man. Quite frankly, I've always thought that he was some unholy demon from the depth." Gran said, with a fierce condemnation.

"I've also been troubled in my spirit as well. I could never seem to shake the disturbing feelings that I got whenever I watched him on television either. He just might be the antichrist." Winn stated in a tone just above a whisper.

I rolled my eyes heavenward. Oh, good grief! I thought. Here we go again. I'm so sick and tired of hearing this stuff. Now it's the Boogie Man! It's always something lurking somewhere around the corner, and it's gonna get'cha if you don't watch out! I eased myself toward the stairs desperately trying to hold back my disdain.

"I'm going bed, I said, straining to keep the irritation out of my voice. Neither of them looked up. They continued their conversation as Winn made her way over to pick up the shards of the potted plant while I went upstairs.

Did they ever give up? I wondered. Can't they just for one day let it go? Of course, a man literally waking up from the dead is a little unnerving, granted. But, maybe the doctors misdiagnosed some underlying condition. Although you can't exactly misdiagnose a stab wound to the head. But, why does it always have to be the end of the world as we know it?

I walked into my bedroom and lay on the bed and stared at the ceiling. I allowed the conversation that we had concerning Grayson's proposal to play through my mind. I was surprised when Gran seemed to understand why I was not ready to give in to such a commitment as marriage. I was not going to be brow-beaten, nor pushed into a situation that I was not prepared for, no matter how aggravated Winn seemed to be. I allowed my mind to mull over the subject for some time before I realized that Winn had come up to her room.

I sighed. Knowing that I needed to talk to her. I love my sister for all of her pushing, and I did not want there to be any animosity between us, especially over Grayson.

I rolled off the bed and walked to her room. I popped my head into the opened door and saw her standing near her vanity.

"Winn," I started. "I hope that you're not too upset with me about ..." I stopped unable to finish my sentence.

She was standing in the middle of the floor, dressed in pajamas and robe, and moving her mouth once again without a sound, and gesturing as if she was speaking to someone directly in front of her. I stifled a small cry with my hand.

I wanted to move toward her, but fear kept me glued in place at the bedroom door. I watched with a dreadful fascination as my sister, oblivious to my presence, begged, implored, and even pleaded with her unseen companion, during the course of this unspoken exchange.

The discourse continued for several seconds then I saw Winn

squint and shield her eyes as if she saw some great, bright, light, flash in front of her. She stood still for a split second and then collapsed to the floor.

"Winn!" I screamed and ran to her.

"What is it?" Gran called from her bedroom.

"I-it's Winn," I yelled back over my shoulder. "S-she's fainted."

I heard movement and sound emanating from the other end of the hall, and then I heard the dull whine of the motor from the wheelchair. Within seconds, Gran had wheeled herself into Winn's room, where I was holding her in my arms.

"What happened?" Gran asked, with an urgent tone of voice.

"Winn...she..." I stumbled, unable to bring myself to say what I saw, or rather what I hadn't seen. "She seems to have had an episode of some sort." I finally resigned to say.

Gran went into the bathroom and returned with a cool washcloth. She handed it to me, and I pressed it against Winn's face and neck and rocked her back and forth as if she was an infant. When her eyes finally fluttered opened, she looked up into a pair of deeply troubled eyes.

"Souline?" she uttered softly. "What happened and why am I on the floor?" The undeniable expression of otherworldliness played within her eyes once again.

"You, uhm...fainted." I gave the only answer I could.

"No, I think you had it right when you said that she had an episode," Gran said. "Are you alright, Baby?" She asked thoughtfully.

"Y-yes ma'am," Winn replied shakily, as I helped her off the floor and onto her bed.

"Did you talk to him again?" Gran asked. My head shot up, and I stared at my Grandmother in absolute astonishment and I gave an involuntary shiver.

"Talk to wh-who?" I asked with trepidation.

Winn and Gran shared a knowing glance, and then they answered in unison, *"The angel."*

"Wh-what?" I stared at them in disbelief. "What are you saying?" My gaze shifted from one and then to the other with some regards to both of their sanity. "Gran, surely you're not telling me that you believe that she has actually been talking to an..., an angel."

"Whether you believe it or not, that's exactly what I've been doing, Souline," Winn confirmed with some irritation.

"Oh, for crying out loud!" I exclaimed impatiently. "You don't honestly expect me to buy into this nonsense about you having these *heavenly encounters.*" I threw up my hands and wriggled my fingers to indicate my skepticism of the eerily supernatural exchange. "Please!" I scoffed at the possibility.

"Yes, I do," she retorted looking up as if the mist was clearing from her eyes.

"Why?" I demanded, greatly annoyed.

"Because," she said quietly. "The message is for you."

"Me?" I exploded, and my eyes flashed with anger. "Excuse me!" I spat out in a derisive tone, my brows furrowed with dark outrage.

"Yes, you," her voice was filled with concern.

"And please tell me, if you can, just what your celestial friend, could possibly have to say to me." I mocked with dripping sarcasm, standing to my feet and crossing my arms defiantly. I glared at her and started to pace the floor.

"That mom was safe," she said quietly.

I spun around on my heels so quickly, I nearly lost my balance.

"What?" I flung the word at Winn and arrogantly looked down my nose at her.

"Mom is safe, Souline," she repeated looking at me from under her lashes, appearing younger and vulnerable somehow.

"I don't think that this is one bit funny, and I'm not going to spend one more minute listening to this mess!" My face was hard and flushed hot with anger. My breast heaved up and down from my aroused resentment. "I'm going to bed!" I marched with black fury toward the door clenching my fist.

"He told me about the *Huntsman*," she added softly.

My breath halted in my breast, and I stopped dead in my tracks. A tiny cry escaped my lips. A slow, pervasive tingle crept up my spine, and I turned and stared at my sister in absolute disbelief. I knew that I had never told her or anyone about that dream.

"H-how d-do you know that?" Anxiety rose in my belly and made a tiny knot.

"I know that he haunts your dreams, Souline," compassion filled her voice and spilled into her eyes.

"Who is the Huntsman, Baby?" Gran saw dread overshadow my face, as I slowly walked back toward my sister.

"I don't know," I muttered in a barely audible whisper.

"But I do," Winn spoke quietly and solemnly.

"How can you? I never told you about that dream. I never understood it enough to tell anyone," I said bemusedly.

"I know, but if you let me, I can tell you what it means," Winn suggested kindly.

"How?" I asked perplexed by the offer.

She said, "The Scriptures say, 'He reveals the deep and secret things: He knows what is in the darkness, and the light dwells with Him.' In other words, God is able to bring all things to light. I'll tell you what the dream means if you want to know."

My eyes were transfixed on Winn's face, and I entreated her to dissect the images and relieve me of the enigmatic phantom that stalked my dreams; a dream that had followed me for most of my life. It was a great weight on my soul, and I did not know why. It would be a tremendous help if I could at least know why it had plagued me. I nodded yes, partly fearful and partly intrigued at the prospect of hearing what my sister would have to say concerning the disturbing enigma.

"I'll tell you the dream," I offered.

"No, I'll tell you," she said, as a puzzled look settled on my face, but I did not argue with her.

A haze of memory filled Winn's eyes as they moved back and forth as if she saw pictures in her mind's eye.

She started. "There is a great mist surrounding you. You're crouching, hiding, from this large man, *The Huntsman*, under a blue and white net."

I gave an involuntary shudder and nod at the accuracy of her interpretation as she began.

"You hear a deafening clap of thunder, but it never rains. You hear the echo of the high shrill of a bird in the distance, and another thunderous boom. Then you hear the heavy footsteps of the Huntsman running toward you, so you crouch still, further underneath the heavy netting, hoping he will not see you.

Floating out of the mist, are giant black, gray, and green birds. But, then they shift and group together like puzzle pieces, and when the pieces are formed, there's no identifiable picture. The footsteps you had heard abruptly stop. He's near. You hold your breath for what seems a lifetime because you think that he might hear or see you. There's a sudden growl that is so loud that it shakes the ground where you're hiding, but you see no animal. Soon the roar of the animal fades away to some distant place, and the Huntsman disappears with it into the night."

I stood astonished and transfixed as she relayed the dream. I felt as if I had been stripped naked, and there was no place to hide and take refuge.

"How do you know this?" I whispered, awestruck and bewildered by the mysterious means by which my sister had so accurately conveyed a detailed account of my dream.

"*He* told me Souline. '*The angel.*'"

I searched her face through tear-filled eyes, still uncertain as to what I could actually believe. However, I could not deny the fact that she had just given me a specific account of a dream that I had never disclosed to anyone. I slumped to the floor with tears rolling down my cheeks, and Gran caressed the back of my head to console me.

"You said that you could tell me what it means," I probed gingerly.

Winn only hesitated for a fraction of a second and then said, "The dream is about Mama."

"Mama?" I shook my head, unable to comprehend." "What do you mean? How is this about Mama?"

"It's about the night..." she choked back her tears and said, "It's about the night she died."

Gran, who had been quiet during the exchange between us, could not hide her curiosity about her daughter-in-law, and eagerly asked, "What about the night Joyceline died?"

"The dream is about how she died," Winn offered solemnly, greatly aware of the air of tension that had settled in the room.

"Remember that night when Mama picked us up here, at Gran's house?" She turned to me and continued. "She had pulled a double shift at the hospital, and she was late collecting us. When she finally picked us up, we were asleep. I have sleepy memories of Granddaddy Joe carrying us out and placing us in the back seat of the SUV. Remember?"

Gran nodded, remembering that night, but not wanting to interrupt Winn's narrative. "On the way home, Mama remembered that we didn't have any milk for breakfast the next morning, so she decided to stop at the convenience store."

I shifted uneasily on the floor, my heart started to pound.

"She pulled into the store parking lot and locked the door, leaving us to sleep in the back seat, just for a moment. She walked into the store not realizing that it was being robbed," Winn continued.

"Oh God, oh God." I hugged myself and started slowly rocking back and forth uncontrollably on the floor with tears running down my face. Winn moved from the bed to sit on the floor next to me, and she enfolded me in her arms as if she was trying to shield me. She saw the look of anguish in my eyes and hugged me.

"The reason you could never figure out your dream, is because it happened to you when you were so young. But, God wanted to help you through this, by revealing your dream to you so that you can learn and overcome the distress you've felt all of these years." She hugged me again.

"Souline, all I'm going to do is unravel the symbols, okay? This is what your dream means. Now, in the dream you're under a blue and white net hiding from the Huntsman, right?"

"Yes, that's right," I spoke quietly, and my mind started on the same journey as my sister's when she began to relay the dream.

"Have you ever wondered why you've always held onto that old crochet blanket of Gran's that she keeps on the sofa for you? I remember one time when she was going to throw it away, and you cried so much that she kept it."

"That's right," Gran said, as she watched and listened. "I had never known you to kick up such a fuss about anything."

"I know, I remember. But what's that got to do with my dream?" I sniffed a little as my tears subsided.

"That evening when Mama picked us up, Gran had covered us with that blanket."

"Yes, I did." Gran nodded in agreement.

"So what..." I looked confused.

"The holes in the crochet stitching of the coverlet Souline, is the net that you were hiding under in your dream." There was a sharp intake of breath as I quickly perceived her meaning.

"That's the blue and white net that I was peeking through," I said as if I had unearthed a great secret. "I woke up when I heard the thunder that night and pulled it over my face. I remember thinking that it was about to storm."

"The thunder that you heard had nothing to do with a storm. Remember, in your dream? You heard thunder, but the rain never came. Instead, you heard the shrill of a bird. The thunder that you heard was a shotgun blast, and the sound of the bird was..." there was a catch in Winn's throat, and she faltered. She looked at me with eyes that held a distinct sorrow and fought the sting of tears that blossomed and brimmed in the corners her eyes.

"What? What was it?" I urged her to tell me because I wanted to know. I desperately wanted to understand this dream that had haunted my sleep and my spirit for most of my life.

"It was Mama. The robber shot one of the other customers, and when she screamed, he shot her which was the other clap of thunder in your dream."

"Oh, no-ooo!" I wailed and started to cry again as the images began to make sense to me. "So the running footsteps that I heard were the footsteps of the man who shot Mama?"

"Yes, Sweetie," she said sympathetically. "And the reason he never saw us was because we were underneath the blanket."

"Well, thank God for that," Gran said softly, realizing the precarious danger her granddaughters had actually been close to that night.

"But what are the giant black, gray, and green birds, or the puzzle pieces that make no picture? I don't understand that."

"Do you remember seeing the jacket or shirt of a man through the holes after you heard the running?" I drew my brows together searching my memory.

"I saw the back of him. That's the reason I scooted down further in the car." My memory was eking out images. "But, I don't..." I shook my head trying to grasp what my sister was telling me.

"Was it a camouflage jacket?" Winn asked.

"Oh, my goodness that's it!" My hand flew to my mouth as I once again understood the meaning of my dream. "The design looked like puzzle pieces to me. But I do remember thinking that the shapes themselves looked like birds to me. Mom was parked next to his car, and I saw the back of his jacket when he ran to the car, but I could not see his face. That's why I heard the footstep that stopped near me. He was getting into the car. But what does the growling animal mean in my dream?"

"The engine was one of those high-performance engines. What you heard was a turbocharged engine speeding away from the scene of a horrible crime."

Before I Wake

I took a long minute to assess what my sister had just told me. Then I placed my head on my knees and wept bitterly. Finally, there was an answer to a storm that had enveloped me for most of my young life. I had wrestled with that dream for as long as I could remember, its meaning always eluded me. I had been very young when Mom died, and I had found it difficult to make sense of the finality of such a great loss.

Initially, no sound emanated from me as I sat on the floor next to Winn rocking back and forth. But, as the dream settled, and I began to comprehend the meaning, I started to cry. My body shook in short spasms that racked my frame that had bowed into a ball. I sat clutching my knees, and the spasms erupted and eventually exploded into a sudden guttural, primal cry. This cry stemmed from a wretched pain that had long been buried in some forgotten grave that lay far within me.

My grandmother and sister moved closer to place their arms about me as if by doing so they could absorb some of the pain. But I could not be consoled at that moment because the pain was so deep. I had unwittingly witnessed the sounds of our mother's murder, and being so young, had not understood and had wrapped them inside of me, and they were manifested through my dreams.

I shed tears that I had kept hidden within me for years; tears that I could not have stopped even if I had wanted to. All of the bewildering fury was now released as I lay in a crumpled mass on my sister's bedroom floor.

The onslaught lasted for a while, and when I recovered, the

questions of why still remained. Why did he kill my mother? Why do people kill? I knew that I might never find the answer to these questions. But I did know that somewhere deep inside, peace would eventually come. Maybe not at this moment, but I knew that someday soon I would be able to put these old specters that haunted me to rest.

"Are you alright, Baby?" Gran asked as she patted the top of my head.

"No," I answered honestly. "But I will be." I gave a watery smile and took another tissue from the box that Winn had handed me.

"Winn had told me about the spiritual exchange that had taken place," Gran said. "I had mentioned to her that I was concerned about her fainting spells. But when she told me what had happened and why she had fainted, I figured that if she had encounters with angels, well, that might cause anyone to give way to fainting. I'm also glad, Souline, that you might have a good chance at finally laying the past to rest. This just might be what you'll need to seek God's help and come to terms with your spiritual well-being."

I said nothing but smiled at my Grandmother. "You better go to bed, Gran, it's very late, and you'll be tired in the morning," I suggested instead.

"Don't worry about me. I just want to make sure everything's alright with you," she said, and gently pulled my ponytail.

"I'll be okay. Go on now and get some sleep." I urged her.

"She'll be okay, Gran," Winn nodded in agreement. "If we need you we'll call."

We both gave her a kiss, and she resigned to a night of

welcomed rest. We heard the gentle whir of the motor as it faded and carried her down the hall to her room.

"Why did he kill her, Winn? He didn't have to do that, did he?"

Winn caressed the top of my head, and simply said, "No, he didn't. But I don't know why he killed her, Sweetie. That was not disclosed to me."

I eyed her speculatively and quietly asked, "Did you really talk to an angel, Winn?"

"Yes, I really did," she gave me a wry smile. I looked at her. I was still grappling with what had just occurred, but I could not argue with the undeniable fact that she not only told me the dream, but she also interpreted the dream as well.

I sighed. "Thank you for helping me to understand."

"Don't thank me, the gift came from God. Remember to thank Him." I said nothing, but smiled and stood to my feet.

"I guess I'd better get to bed myself. It's been a rather eventful evening for us all.

"You don't believe me, do you, Souline?" Winn asked, giving me a doubtful look.

I looked at Winn in earnest and said, "I don't know what to believe right now."

"It's important that you do, believe me, Souline," she stood and faced me soberly.

"Why?" I asked noting the grave look that had settled on my sister's face.

"There is another part to the message that I received, that I didn't want to mention while Gran was here."

"Why not?" My heart quickened for some unknown reason.

"This part of the message had nothing to do with the dream. I wanted to speak to you alone," she said seriously. "The angel told me that Christ's return was imminent and that you would not be part of His initial return. But, the messenger said for you not to lose heart, that if you hold fast and keep the faith, in the end you would endure and conquer."

I looked at her, not sure what I should say. "Winn, what are you talking about? What does that mean?"

"It means that Christ is coming soon to gather his children from every corner of the earth. He's coming a lot sooner than even believers realize. Once this happens, the earth will undergo events that have been foretold by the prophets, since the beginning of time."

"You're talking about the Rapture aren't you?"

"Yes. Once the believers of Christ are taken from the earth, mankind will experience horrendous, catastrophic events unlike anything the world as ever known. So you must prepare yourself." She reached for a book that lay on her bed, "Here, take my Bible, Souline."

Winn," I protested when she handed it to me.

"Let it be your guide, it will not fail you if you allow it to direct your heart." She continued. "There are going to be unprecedented occurrences that will befall the entire human race, and there will be nowhere to escape. There is a chance that you will endure unthinkable horrors at the hand of a dictator in a *One World Religious System*. Do not take his mark and fight him, Souline, fight him and his kind with everything you've got. Fight him with the word of God and with your whole heart, body, and soul. Because, quite frankly if you don't fight, it will be to your spiritual detriment and your soul's damnation."

She grabbed my shoulders and compelled me to look at her. "If there's one thing I know about you, Souline it's that you're a fighter. Don't give up. Do you hear me? Fight!" she said shaking my shoulders. "Fight!"

I looked at my sister, bewildered, tired, weary and a little unsettled by her manner. I was mentally and physically drained, and I did not feel like arguing with her. I handed her back the book that she had thrust into my hands and said, "I'll get this in the morning. Right now I'm just too tired. Okay? Goodnight." I hugged her and walked toward the door.

"There is a way out," Winn said.

"Winn, please, I'm just tapped out."

"Accept Christ now for the atonement of your sins," she stated simply.

I offered her a tired smile and said, "I'll think about it. Right now, I'm just too tired to think about anything but sleep."

I walked to my room and got ready for bed. I was glad for the darkness that had waited to envelop me, glad for the quiet that caressed and embraced me and glad for the hope that I could finally settle into sleep.

CHAPTER FOURTEEN

Two women shall be grinding at the mill; the one shall be taken, and the other left

Math 24:41 (KJV)

6:13 a.m. Friday, June 14, 20__

Sleep had not come easy for me the night before. I tried to rest there in the dark, but there was an uneasy feeling that had settled around me that I could not resolve. I had tossed and turned, most of the night. How did Winn know about that dream? Had she really talked to an angel? Did she really have some connection with a heavenly being? If so, what did it all mean? What exactly did that cryptic message mean, from her angelic host? She had said that I would endure and conquer. Did this really have something to do with my spiritual life, regarding end time prophecy?

Stories about end time prophecy made the hairs stand up on my arms. I remembered feeling uncomfortable when I was a child, and to be honest, I was always a little frightened by it all. My family would always seem elated, even joyful at the prospect of the world's end and I would walk away feeling uneasy and confused. Why were things in life sometimes so difficult? I sighed and sat up in the bed. I heroically fought an overwhelming urge to call in sick. By the time I finally got dressed and ready for work, I was late getting downstairs for breakfast. I finished off my toast and orange juice just as Grayson drove up and honked his horn. I yelled goodbye over my shoulder to my family and made an ungraceful dash to the car.

"Good morning, Sweetheart," was Grayson's cheerful greeting.

"Hey," I said tiredly.

"Another late night?" he inquired. "And please note that it's not my fault this time."

I smiled at him. "Weird was more like it."

"Oh? Weird how?" He steered the car away from the curb.

I hesitated at first and then the story just spilled out of me.

"I know what I'm going to say is going to sound...well bizarre. But, do you remember what I told you about Winn's... uhm, episode?"

"Episode?" He let his mind travel back to the conversation we had yesterday, and recognition washed over his face. "You mean that *angel* thing?"

"Yeah, that angel thing. Well, we had a full blown encounter last night, and it was a doozy. Apparently I was the reason for his mission."

"You?" Grayson could not hide the astonishment in his voice or on his face.

"Yes," I confirmed and plunged into the details of what took place the night before, up to and including the dream revelation. I watched his reaction to the tale with as much interest as he seemed to have in listening to the account. When I finished, he let go his customary long, low whistle.

"Was she right?" he asked with unabashed interest. "About the dream I mean?"

"Yes," I answered soberly. "Every single word. That's what is so disconcerting about all of this. I never told anyone about the dream."

"Are you sure? Maybe you told her about it, and you just forgot."

"No," I reply emphatically. "I never talked about the dream to her, not to you, not anyone. So how could she know, Gray?"

He shrugged his shoulders and said, "I don't know, Honey."

He cast a brief glance toward me. "So it was about the night that you actually saw the man who murdered your mom?"

"I just saw his back." I corrected.

"I'm sorry, Sweetheart," he freed a hand from the steering wheel and kissed the back of my hand. "What can I do to help?"

"Oh, I'm okay," I said. "It's just going to take a while for me to sort out things, but thanks for the offer." I smiled, and there was a short silence in the car that was broken when I asked, "Do you think that it's possible, that she could have actually spoken to an angel?"

"I don't know, Honey, but then, who am I? I suppose anything is possible.

Before I Wake

1:18 p.m.: Friday, June 14, 20__

I was distracted at intervals during the school day. My mind kept wandering back to the cryptic statement that Winn had made the night before. Winn said that the angels message was, *'Don't lose heart but in the end you will endure and conquer.'* The words played over and over in my mind like a hollow echo. To endure implied that I was going to go through some ordeal, and to conquer suggested a battle. She said, *'If there's one thing I know about you, it's that you're a fighter. Don't give up, do you hear me! Fight!* Endure, conquer, fight… What was she talking about? What did all of this mean?

When the school day finally came to a close, I gave a sigh of relief. I loved my job, but this week had proven to be particularly trying, and I was glad that I had the weekend ahead of me so that I could get some rest.

3:18 p.m.: Friday, June 14, 20__

I walked outside expecting to see Grayson's sedan. Instead, Winn was waiting for me in the van.

"Hey," I smiled and waved as I walked toward the parked vehicle. "What are you doing here?" I asked, moving papers and sheet music from the passenger's seat to the back so that I could sit comfortably.

"I ran into Grayson downtown today at lunch time. He said that he was going to help a couple close on their home this afternoon. He thought he might be a little late picking you up, so I volunteered to bring you home. It's been awhile since I've picked up my little sister," she gave an impish giggle.

"Thanks," I laughed and lifted myself up onto the seat of the van. Friday afternoon traffic was usually dreadful, and today was no exception. I never thought of Summerville as a big city, not by the furthest stretch of the imagination, but sometimes it had the feel of a metropolis, especially when traffic was bumper to bumper.

"I keep saying I'm going to get me one of those GPS navigational systems, but you know how I hate gadgets." Winn's cute head bobbed up and down, and in and out, as she hummed and inched her way to merge into downtown traffic.

"You're just old fashioned," I teased.

"I know, but so are you, for all of your artsy-bohemian ways, dear sister." She smiled, and we both broke into laughter.

Winn started softly singing, *Jesus Keep Me Near the Cross*, as she weaved in and out of traffic. I smiled at her. She would always sing as a way of dealing with stress whenever she became nervous or anxious.

"You want to wait the traffic out by grabbing something to eat?" she asked.

"Sure," I smiled and nodded at the agreeable idea.

Winn inched her way down Main Street for three blocks, turned left onto Market Street, which was a lot less congested, and drove about a quarter of a mile until we arrived at *The Nautical House*.

The Nautical House was a quiet, sophisticated, restaurant that had a chic atmosphere and as the name suggested, the restaurant harbored boating or seaworthy paraphernalia on its walls and tables, and was nestled on the exclusive south shore along the riverside of downtown Summerville. We were seated at a small square table, that donned a dark navy linen tablecloth, and pristine white napkins that were folded into beautiful cloth swans, and placed in the center of each blue and white setting."

"Hi, I'm Nita, I'll be serving you today," smiled the young waitress. She was an attractive college student, dressed in a navy uniform and white apron, with tiny braided hair that spilled out of her oversized mud cloth headband. She was kind and friendly and even joked with us while we ordered our appetizer. After she had returned with our drinks and appetizers, we sat and talked about the workday and continued until Nita brought in our main course. It had been some time since we had sat and talked and laughed this way. We had always been close, but lately we had been running in different directions and had just not found time to sit and enjoy the pleasure of each other's company. We deliberately steered our conversation away from the encounter of the night before. I think Winn respected the fact that I needed time to work things out in my mind and understood that she didn't need to push her opinions on me at this moment. I smiled at my sister's exaggerated antics, as she expressed a story that had happened between her, and one of her co-workers, earlier that morning. As I watched Winn's animated gestures, a palpable, poignant, sense of foreboding touched me. It was as if I was saying goodbye to her. I shivered inwardly and fought an absurd urge to cry. The feeling was fleeting, and I shrugged it off.

"Are you okay?" Winn stopped and asked when she observed the momentary lapse in concentration, dart across my face.

"Oh, sure, I'm good," I patted her hand to reassure her.

"Well, I guess we need to start for home anyway, I said as we were finishing up our meal. I caught Nita's attention and asked for the check. I'll call Gran, and let her know that we're on our way."

The drive home was not nearly as nerve-wracking as it had been earlier. The snarled traffic had eased, and the streets were more maneuverable, as Winn made her way toward Thrushwood.

I had never been so glad to see home. I dropped my tote bag near the door of my bedroom and glanced at the clock on my dressing table. It was only a quarter before five, but it seemed longer I thought, as I sat on the edge of the bed.

"Thank God, it's the weekend," a habitual sigh escaped my lips, and I got up to go downstairs.

I walked into the kitchen, to get a glass of water, and my mind raced back to the night before. I was still struck by the fact that Winn was able to tell me about the dream with great accuracy, not to mention the fact that she had deciphered each element of the incident with such detail. I was still not completely sold on the idea that she was able to unravel the dream with the help of a resident of heaven. I knew that she was not a liar, but I just was not ready to give credence to such an incredible notion. I gave a slight chuckle, happy that I could find a little humor in a situation that I could not have laughed about last night.

"Angels, really?" I uttered and shook my head, as I closed the refrigerator door after pouring water from the pitcher.

"Still don't believe me, do you?

I whipped around quickly, and water sloshed over my hand

from the glass I was holding. I had not heard Winn enter the kitchen.

"I wish you wouldn't do that, you scared the heebie-jeebies out of me."

"Sorry," Winn grinned when she saw my startled expression and handed me a paper towel. "Were you thinking about what I told you last night?"

"Wouldn't you? It's been going over and over in my mind, all day." I confessed, wiping the water from my hand.

"Yeah, I guess it would be on my mind too," she stated earnestly. She looked me squarely in the eye and asked, "Souline, why didn't you ever tell anyone about the dream?"

"Oh, I don't know," I started slowly. I absently stared at the floor and slid my foot back and forth across the white tile, as I thought about the harsh imagery of the dream. "I wasn't sure about the dream myself. What I mean is, I didn't understand it, so how was I going to explain it to someone else?"

She nodded and said, "I see. That must have been such a burden for you to carry. I mean about Mama's death, and everything. But now you'll start to heal."

"I know. I just have to work things out." I reached over and hugged her, and we held on to each other, with an understanding that comes from a lifetime of shared experiences. I knew that our spirits were knitted together in a way that could not be separated by time or space. I was glad that I had journeyed through the world with this soul. She had made my voyage much easier than had I traveled it alone, and I found myself hoping that I had done the same for her.

Once again, the feeling as if I were saying goodbye to her washed over me as I hugged her, and when the embrace ended we smiled at each other. I walked over to the sink and turned raising a finger to question her.

"Uhm, I did want to ask you one thing..."

"Sure," she beamed.

"What did you mean when you said that I wouldn't be a part of the initial return, but that I would endure and conquer?"

Her countenance fell a little, and she turned and walked toward me. She grabbed my hand and patted it and was about to answer when her head snapped up, and she scanned the room as if she heard an unexpected sound. She was slightly puzzled.

"Did you hear that?" she asked, still holding my hand.

"Hear, what?" I replied, wondering if she was about to have another one of her episodes.

"Someone shouting." Then she gave a short intake of breath, "Oh my God, do you see them? How beautiful!" She said breathlessly and in a rapturous tone. "There are thousands of them all around us." Her eyes scanned the room as if she could see beyond my scope.

"Winn, what are you talking about?" I stared at her, a little unnerved by her behavior.

"There are angles everywhere! They are so beautiful." She uttered absolutely awestruck.

"Winn, this isn't fun..."

"Shhhh, do you hear the trumpet? Don't you hear..."

"What are you talking..." I never finished the question and

neither did she. Just then there was an incredible sensation that can only be described as *LOVE* came from Winn's hand and rushed through my entire body, like and electrical current. I had never felt anything like it in my life. It was pure unadulterated *LOVE*. It was so overwhelming at first that I staggered against the kitchen counter.

Then a few seconds later, there was a flash of light and the deafening sound of the shattered glass that had fallen from my hand that rang in my ears. Stunned and shaken, I felt the contents splatter across my legs when it struck the floor.

I blinked and stared in disbelief, as the essence of my sister's viability vanished before my eyes. I felt the warmth of her hand fade away. What started as a stifled cry, increased and then erupted into a vociferous and uncontrollable, involuntary scream. The scream seemed to reach out into eternity and reverberate into a deep space that echoed beyond the room.

"Winn!" I screamed and carried the hand that she had been holding to my lips.

"Winn!" I stupidly searched the kitchen, unable to grasp the surreal thought of her literally disappearing right in front of me. I ran into the living room, searching for her and screamed her name once more. "Winn!"

"Gran!" The call was primal, course, and guttural. "Gran!" I called again and bound up the steps, and ran to her bedroom. She was nowhere to be found. I frantically searched the other rooms, as tears caused by the anxiety, started to flow from my eyes.

Maybe she went next door to Miss Ida's while we were in the

kitchen, I thought. I hurried back down the steps and stopped in my tracks; just before I reached the bottom of the stairs, I noticed something peculiar. At first it had not registered when I took the initial flight up the stairs, but I turned and realized that Gran's chair lift was in between floors. When I saw the clothes she had been wearing resting on the lift, and her shoes left on the steps, an inexplicable panic struck me.

I dashed back into the kitchen and looked where Winn had been standing. My hand flew to my mouth, and I let out another small cry of anguish. I stooped down, reached for the blouse that Winn had been wearing, but I could not bring myself to pick it up. My hand shook uncontrollably. Heighten anxiety caused my breathing to become laborious. I backed away and ran into the living room to phone Gray.

"Hello, Grayson Garrett speaking," the deep voice resonated on the other end.

"Gray!" I knew I sounded wild and excited.

"Souline?" he queried.

"W-Winn...Winn's gone! I saw her, but she's not there. I-I was holding her hand." I was crying and screeching, in my frenzied state of mind.

"Souline?" He questioned again, but I was not listening

"They, s-she, she's gone and I can't find Gran either!" I was nearly screaming over the phone.

"Souline, Baby calm down! Listen..." He tried once more but to no avail. "Honey, please listen...I'm supposed to show this couple a house, but I'll reschedule and be over in about fifteen minutes. Okay? Do you hear me? Souline, just calm down!" He was yelling, but I wasn't listening to him. I wanted to find my grandmother to tell her what had happened to Winn.

"Gray, Winn is gone and I need to find Gran!"

"Souline!" He yelled. "Soul...."

I hung up.

The thought that my grandmother may have been next door, at Miss Ida's, recurred to me. I ran out of the house in a flurry toward the Jackson's house. I was past the point of reason in my desperation to find my family. I ran out into the front yard and nearly knocked down Mr. Jackson, who was on his way over to see if his wife was next door at our house. Later, I would come to the realization that both my grandmother's wheelchairs, were still in the house, and even later still before I would admit to myself, that I would never see my family again.

CHAPTER FIFTEEN

In a moment in the twinkling of an eye.

1 Corinthians 15:52 (KJV)

5:12 p.m. Friday, June 14, 20___

The reception areas of the local television and news radio stations became inundated with calls from the Summerville community, with bizarre occurrences and reports of vanishing family, friends, and co-workers just as the city's rush hour began. The receptionist at the Channel Five television station had answered a call from a woman, who said that her friend had disappeared right before her eyes while she was talking with her.

The receptionist thanked the woman for the information in her best professional voice, said that she would get someone to look into the incident, and hung up the phone. Just at that moment, one of the local news personalities walked past her desk, and she relayed the message to him. They both made snide remarks and gestures indicating that the woman was either drunk or crazy, and they had a good laugh at the woman's expense. But had the woman caller known that she was the object of ridicule she would have had the last laugh; because at that very moment, both the receptionist and the reporter heard the managing editor of the newsroom release a blood-curdling scream and dash down the stairs insisting that she saw not one, but two of their copywriters vanish right in front of her.

The phone rang again.

"News Channel Five, may I help you?" The receptionist said soberly.

"Hello." A youthful male voice, that sounded as if he might have been in his early twenties, spoke on the other end of the phone. He was not overly excited, in fact, he sounded rather nonchalant about the matter. "I know that you're not going to believe me when I tell you this, but I was out walking my dog in the park, and I saw this couple out for an afternoon run, just vanish, like *poof*, right in front of me. Their clothes were left right where they were running. I know it sounds crazy, and, believe me, I don't even make calls like this, but I think that maybe someone should kinda look into this. Okay? Well, thanks."

The line went dead and this time the receptionist, who appeared to be in a mild state of shock, did not laugh. The smug tone had vanished from her voice. It seemed that one of the copywriters that had disappeared was her best friend.

Across town, Summerville's afternoon commute was brutal. Tempers flared as downtown traffic began to mount for a second time that afternoon. Reluctant travelers began to thrust their way through the mass of conveyances trying to reach their afternoon destinations.

There was a sudden screech of breaks and horrendous crashes

of metal and the sound of several automobiles that were unable to stop in time to avoid the intermingling mass of vehicles. The woman whose car caused one of the crashes, jumped out of her car in violent agitation, screaming hysterically that her husband had just disappeared from behind the wheel of their car.

About a block west of this accident, an angry driver from public works inadvertently struck an automobile that had suddenly stopped in the middle of the road. When the mid-sized silver car that was struck finally spun to a stop, it was facing in the opposite direction of traffic after skidding a few feet. The public works driver, who looked as if he had never missed a meal, jumped down from the cab of the truck, headed toward the car, walking as if he might leave potholes on the pavement, and began mumbling under his breath what he was about to say to the unfortunate driver of the silver automobile.

"All right, buddy, why would you stop in the middle of the street like that?" The harsh, gruff, voice ground out. "When I get my hands on you, I'm gonna beat the..." He stopped short, as he reached the car and tried to jerk the door of the automobile open, only to find it was locked. "What the...?" he barked, adding a liberal sprinkling of expletives. He lifted his hat and scratched his head as he quickly scanned his surroundings, with some confusion. He looked out across the intersection and then back into the car, greatly puzzled. What the truck driver found, to his amazement, was the fact that the driver of the silver automobile was nowhere in sight. He only saw the clothing of an adult female scattered across the front seat, and the clothing of what seemed to be two younger children interspersed across the back seat. Although though the car had been struck, the motor of the vehicle was still idling. Where were the occupants? He wondered.

At that moment throughout the city, onlookers heard and saw simultaneous crashes and explosions occur. There was one incident whereby a school bus transporting elementary children ran head-long into an office building. When the accident was reported and investigated, none of the occupants including the bus driver were ever found.

Another incident occurred when an airplane skidded along the tops of a series of buildings and shops just before it crashed into a ten story bank building and burst into flames. At this same moment, there were chaotic cries from people in the general vicinity of downtown, running for protective cover or running to see if they could offer assistance in a sundry of other accidents that had started to take place all over the city. There were also articles of clothing and personal belongings that had been left by their owners in heaps on the many streets and sidewalks of Summerville, where the occupants, walking to and from their destinations, had dispensed of their possessions in a rather unorthodox manner.

Traffic on the interstate had now come to a complete stop. A number of vehicles in both north and southbound lanes had run off embankments or crashed through railings. Some cars had crossed lanes into oncoming traffic or were found heading in the opposite direction on the highway without their drivers. One tractor-trailer that was traveling at about seventy-five miles per hour failed to slow down when traffic started to halt. The truck plowed into several automobiles, overturned several times, skidded and landed on its side, resting contrary to traffic on the roadway. It was carrying boxes of office supplies that were thrown out and scattered across the highway for several feet.

Many of the drivers who had managed to escape the collision ran to help other travelers that had not been so lucky. Several people vanished into thin air while running to help the victims who were in the crash. When the few people that remained climbed onto the trailer and opened the door, they discovered there was no driver in the cab of the overturned truck. It was observed in hundreds of the cars that were left on the highway that many of their owners had gone missing.

Calls of astronomical proportion started filtering into Summerville's emergency services about the incidents and accidents from all over the city. The most urgent of these calls were from people swearing they had witnessed the vanishings of family, friends, and co-workers.

In the Gourmet Griddle, a handsome man in his early thirties, waiting for his wife, glanced at his watch once again with some concern because she had been in the powder room for some time. He was just about to ask the head waitress if she would go in and check on her when, Vickie, a young brunette waitress, came from the restroom carrying a pair of black slacks, a white blouse, lingerie, a handbag, a wedding ring and a beautiful black lace vintage shawl.

"Where did you get that?" the man asked accusingly, pointing to the shawl he had bought his wife for her birthday about a year ago, as Vickie passed his table.

"It was in the bathroom, on the floor. I was bringing it..."

"That belongs to my wife," he cut her off and grabbed the garment, eyeing the waitress suspiciously. "Where is she?" He demanded, shaking the garment at her as he snatched his wife's handbag from her hands as well.

"There's no one in there, sir," the waitress said, mildly, although she resented the haughty, suspicious, attitude of the patron.

"What do you mean, there's no one in there? I'm sure she didn't just vanish into thin air, and she certainly could not leave without her clothes," he said agitated, grabbing his wife's remaining possessions from the waitress. "Sharron...Sharron, honey!" He called to his wife, his agitation increasing as he ran toward the bathroom door, with shawl and belongings in hand, and with both waitresses following close behind. When the door was thrown open, it was as the waitress had said.

There was no one there.

Simultaneously, at The Nautical House, an over-excitable chef was screaming at one of the waiters for returning two of the dinners he had just prepared. The eccentric chef was insulted that his food was being returned. Finally, the waiter calmed the impatient chef long enough to explain to him, that the couple who had been sitting at his station had vanished right in front of him just as he was bringing them their dinner. The chef became so incensed and frustrated at what he interpreted as a fabrication, that he threw both the dinners at the waiter just as he escaped through the kitchen doors.

A patron on the other side of the room was startled into hysterics, dropped her coffee cup, and screamed when the coffee pot that her pert little waitress was carrying, literally teetered in mid-air just before it smashed to the floor. The waitress had disappeared into thin air, leaving her order booklet, navy uniform, white apron, shoes, and a mud cloth headband that she was wearing around her small, braided head.

Mrs. Solomon, the owner of *Happy Land Daycare*, was slightly annoyed with Lisa Armstrong, a young mother, who was late picking up her three rambunctious boys that afternoon. They were good boys, but they had been more than a handful for the staff that day. It was Friday, and everyone was anxious to start their weekend, so Mrs. Solomon told her other staff members they could leave, and she would wait for the boys' mother. As soon as she saw the young mother, Mrs. Solomon started spouting her pre-rehearsed rhetoric about the boys' behavior, even before the harried woman could get through the playground gate. Justin was helping his younger brother Samuel up into a swing while his twin Austin, was on his way down the sliding board.

"Hi, Mommy! Loo'kat me!" Austin called to his mother as he dashed down the slide, this time on his stomach.

"I'm sorry, Mrs. Solomon, I'll speak to the boys when we get home. They're good boys; it's just that since their father left, they've been a little difficult to control," she apologized.

"Come on boys, it's time to go!" She yelled to her sons across the playground and Austin started running toward her.

"Humph, I'm sure," Mrs. Solomon said with a sniff.

"Hi, Mommy." The boy patted her and smiled up at the young woman who looked worn and tired and older than her years. She managed a smile that brightened her eyes and added a bit of youth back to her face as she bent down to hug her small son.

"Hello, Sweetheart," she said and kissed the top of his auburn head. Justin was still pushing his younger brother, Samuel in the swing.

"Come on boys! Don't keep your mother waiting," the older woman said rather testily and with a fake smile. "There is a late fee you know, Mrs. Armstrong. It is due on the day that the extra expenses are incurred, and of course in your case it will be multiplied by three," the older woman stated, emphasizing her annoyance with the young mother for being late.

"Yes, I-I know, Lisa hedged. "I just don't have the money with me, today. Could I pay you Monday?"

Mrs. Solomon stiffened her back and looked down her nose at the younger woman. Lisa looked crestfallen, not sure where she would get the extra money to pay the added expense.

"Mrs. Armstrong," Mrs. Solomon rolled out haughtily as she folded her arms over her ample bosom, "The fees are really due on the day that you are late. You know this."

"I know... it's just that traffic was so heavy, and I am barely making ends meet as it is, and I need to..."

The last thing that Mrs. Solomon saw before she slipped into a misty fog and hit the ground, were four extraordinary flashes of light, four piles of clothing left by their previous owners, and the movement of an empty swing on the playground.

When Mrs. Solomon came to, she knew that she would never receive the late fee from Mrs. Armstrong.

Walter Sterling was driving his regular bus route through the downtown business district when traffic started to get ugly. He had been driving public transportation for almost twenty-five years, so he knew that the demands of the job could often be trying even to the most experienced driver. Traffic was starting to crawl and he was trying to make it to Market and Broad so that his passengers would not miss the 5:25 p.m. connection, but he soon realized that it was not going to happen. He also had a bus that was packed to standing capacity.

"Man, it's rough going this afternoon," an older man in his early seventies sitting directly across from the bus driver said, as the bus inched through the congestion.

"Yeah," said the driver, concentrating on the traffic ahead. "I don't know if I'm going to make the next connection in time."

"Well you better do something," the testy reply came from a young black woman who looked to be in her early twenties. She was sitting in the seat to the left of the older gentleman and had broken in on the conversation. "I can't afford to be late to my job," she drawled. "And if I miss that connection it's gonna be too bad."

The bus driver smiled and said, "I'll do my best."

"Humph," she huffed. "Somebody better do something..."

The older gentlemen smiled and said, "Well, there's quite a bit of traffic out this afternoon, young lady."

"But, I wasn't talking to you," she said, with a cluck of her tongue, as she rolled her eyes and neck simultaneously and glared at the elderly man.

"Hey now, let's not be disrespectful," the bus driver said reproachfully and looked up in his mirror to catch the eye of the young woman.

"All-llll I'm saying is..." she drawled and raised an index finger, with one excessively long acrylic nail, and started on a tirade about not getting to work on time and not wanting to explain to her boss why she missed her connection.

Before I Wake

Heavy sighs were emitted from some of the other passengers on the bus as she continued to elaborate her concerns about her untimely circumstances. Some were listening to the conversation, some were pretending not to hear the dispute, others just wanted to get through the commute without incident, but most were just tired and wanted to get home.

The bus driver had asked the young woman what bus was she trying to connect with, and was in the process of calling a fellow driver over the dispatch radio to request that he wait about five minutes so that he could get the young lady there in time to catch the bus; when a piercing scream from one of the passengers near the back, filled the bus. Everyone one on the bus quickly turned their heads to see what caused the commotion. A woman in her mid-thirties had jumped up and pointed at the seat next to her, but not before more than one-third of the passengers on the bus disappeared. There were several audible intakes of breath, and then a palpable silence that ran among the passengers, to indicate their shock and disbelief.

The young woman, who had been arguing with the bus driver, looked up just in time to see the bus crash into a dry cleaning van that was just inches in front of the bus. The older man that had been seated next to her looked at her and offered an apologetic smile and vanished, with a flash of light, into thin air. She then noticed the dangling radio receiver that the bus driver had been holding swinging from its base, and saw his uniform, as well as the paraphernalia of several other passengers that had been standing on the bus scattered on the seats and floor. She looked around the now sparse bus, realized the mounting confusion that was about to take place, spat out an expletive and said with disgust, "I'm gonna be late for work."

At the *Westwood Funeral Home*, the newly widowed Mrs. Richard Williams III stood over the casket of her husband, sobbing as she touched the cool lifeless hand of her deceased loved one. Stephanie Williams-Archer, who was one year older than her stepmother, gave her brother Anthony a cold side glance as she stood, impatiently watching the young widow weep.

"Oh for God's sake, Tammy!" she snapped. "He's dead. He left you all of the money, so you don't have to pretend anymore." Stephanie violently spat out the words, obviously agitated with the beautiful blond who caressed her husband's hand.

"This is not the place, Steph," Anthony placed a hand under his sister's elbow to remind her where she was.

"I know you never believed that I loved your father, but I did," Tammy retorted softly, through the black mourning veil. "I loved him very much. He was so kind to me." The young woman sniffed into a beautiful white lace handkerchief.

"Oh, please," Stephanie sneered derisively.

"Steph, please," her brother implored, glancing around the room that was filled to capacity with mourners who came to pay their last respects and who began to notice his sister's exaggerated tones.

Stephanie snatched her elbow away from her brother's hand and was about to heatedly round on him to express her indignation when Tammy let out an unearthly shriek that made the heads of even the most inattentive of mourners snap to attention. Tammy was shaking with bewilderment and fear, as she stared and pointed at the empty navy blue suit, now devoid of her husband whose hand she had been caressing, and who had been lying there a few seconds ago.

"Oh my God!" Stephanie's hand flew to her mouth when she observed the empty casket that had once held her father. Anthony and one of the ushers caught Stephanie just before she slipped to the floor as she fainted. But no one caught Anthony when Tammy, the usher, and about three-fourths of the mourners in the chapel disappeared into thin air.

Nine-year-old Shelly Carlton was dreading her walk past Jennifer Parkinson's house on her way to her piano lessons. When Shelly had to walk alone, she usually took the long way around to her teacher, Mrs. Blackwell's home. However, today her older brother had been held up at baseball practice and was not able to walk her to her lessons as he had promised. Now, she was late and was obliged to take the shorter route past the Parkinson's house so that her mother would not be upset with her for her tardiness. Mrs. Carlton was always reminding Shelly that if she was paying for an hour lesson, she wanted her to be responsible and be on time for piano practice. She saw the living room curtains move and knew that Jennifer had been watching her draw near the Parkinson's home.

"God please, God please, God please help me," she started her mantra, and Shelly quickened her steps as she approached the house, but to no avail.

"Where ya' goin', Smelly-Shelly?" the rather plump, redhead Jennifer called as she flew out of the house and jumped off the porch, running toward her in a manner resembling a junior linebacker. Shelly tried to ignore the girl but knew from past experiences that it never worked.

"Hey!" The large freckled faced girl yelled, as she lumbered toward the slender brunette. "You hear me talkin' to you!"

"I've got to go, Jennifer. I'm going to be late for my lessons," Shelly said, her voice shaking as nervously as the rest of her body.

"I'm going to be late for my lessons." Jennifer scrunched up her face and mocked her, knocking the sheet music out of her hands. Shelly stooped to pick up the sheets of paper, and the large girl grabbed and yanked one of her ponytails with malevolent vigor.

"Stop it, Jennifer!" Shelly said, desperately trying to put on a brave face but failing miserably.

"Or what? You're gonna tell your big brother on me? Well, he don't scare me either. He can bring it on, too. I'll take on both of you at the same time." Shelly shot her a rather doubtful look, realizing it was an empty threat. She tried to go around the large girl, but her music went flying again when Jennifer pushed her.

Shelly stumbled backward toward the earth, but she did not quite fall. Just before she was about to hit the ground, Shelly vanished right in front of a very surprised and very frightened Jennifer Parkinson.

The large girl ran screaming into the house to relay her side of the story to Mrs. Parkinson. Jennifer swearing that she did not do anything to cause Shelly's disappearance. But just before Shelly vanished, Jennifer would have sworn that she heard a very grateful Shelly say, "Thanks, God."

Paul Dunaway, a manager of a local fast food franchise, was having a heated conversation with his son, James, who was in his junior year of college while they were driving on their way home.

Before I Wake

"Dad, I don't want to go into the food business when I graduate. I want to be a writer," said James, emphatically.

"Son, it's good, steady work, and writing won't pay the bills. I think that if you...what in the world?" Mr. Dunaway slammed on his brakes just as he was making a right turn onto Amsterdam, which is the site of the Summerville National Cemetery. All at once birds that had filled the trees took flight and spread through the open sky like a great black mist. Suddenly, the ground began to shake violently beneath them.

The quake was strong enough to topple several of the larger trees that were in the area, to shatter glass and burst a gas line beneath the street a few miles down the road. Mr. Dunaway, along with several others who were driving on the same road, had to slam on their brakes to keep from crashing into each other.

"Dad, look!" When the quake subsided, James pointed, astonished by what he was witnessing. Mr. Dunaway had parked the car, and they both jumped out and stared in disbelief.

They saw hundreds of the graves literally split open at once and watched, as many of their residents seemed to be spirited away on the wind. There was an odd mingling of forms and mist that seem to float upward on a stream of air and light. The shocked father and son, first stared at each other and then looked around at some of the other spectators standing nearby that had stopped near the cemetery, and who were just as awestruck by what they had just seen. Each one staring from person to person as if trying to confirm if they had really witnessed the phenomenon. At that very moment, there was a simultaneous sharp intake of breath, from both father and son, when several of the people that had been standing around disappeared leaving only their garments behind.

What had happened?

That was the question that was asked by millions on that day of days when the world held its breath for one brief moment.

CHAPTER SIXTEEN

Wake up, O sleeper, rise from the dead.

Ephesians 5:14 (NIV)

4:02 p.m. Saturday, June 15, 20__

What had happened?

At that moment, echoes of the once living, danced past many of the residences of Summerville, as millions upon millions of the world's population moved beyond this realm that fateful afternoon. There was not a place on earth, where some soul that had once occupied a place in someone's home, someone's heart or someone's life, had not gone missing that day.

I sat on the edge of the bed idly riffling the edges of Winn's Bible. When I picked the book up, a white envelope slipped from its pages to the floor. As I reached for it, I noticed my sister's handwriting scrawled across the front of the stark white enclosure. It simply said Souline. I opened the paper rectangle and read the letter. Astonished by its content, tears streamed down my cheeks, and I pulled my knees close to my body and rocked back and forth while I read.

I read the letter a second time and this time I opened the Bible to the Scriptures that Winn had requested me to read in the missive. As I did, a small beam of clarity penetrated the muddle that had settled in my thoughts, since the beginning of the occurrence.

"Souline?" An anxious call from downstairs shook me from my thought process.

"Yes, I'm here Gray, in Winn's room." I sniffed and wiped my eyes with the back of my hand. I heard him bound up the stairs, rapidly overtaking the passage.

"Sweetheart, I've been worried sick about you. What have you been doing?" He looked greatly relieved and gave me a hug.

"I've just been going over things in my mind, trying to understand what happened," I stated simply.

"I don't think anybody knows just exactly what happened. Quite frankly, we may never know." He sat next to me on the bed.

"Winn tried to tell me, and I just wouldn't listen." A great sigh of regret escaped from me.

"Honey, you're not going to start that again are you?"

"It's right here." I opened up the Bible where Winn had dog-eared a corner. Here, read it."

"Souline..." he started.

"I'll read it," I said," anxious for him to understand. "First Thessalonians 4:16 'For the Lord himself shall descend from heaven with a shout, with the voice of the archangel, and with the trump of God: and the dead in Christ shall rise first: Then we which are alive and remain shall be caught up together with them in the clouds, to meet the Lord in the air.'"

For the second time that day I had given him that imploring look.

"Don't you see, Gray? This is what she was trying to tell me. I just didn't believe her."

"Souline, I just can't get behind all of this slight-of-hand mumbo-jumbo," he said evenly.

"Do you have any other explanation for everything that has happened?" I asked pointedly.

"No. But, I can't believe that you are trying to rationalize this experience with this passage."

"Just before Winn..." I took a deep breath and allowed myself to face the possible truth of my sister's departure. I said evenly and started again slowly. "Just before Winn vanished, we were talking, and she asked me if I'd heard someone shout, and if I heard a trumpet. Of course, I hadn't, but before I could answer her question she was gone."

"Yes, so what's that got to do with anything? He asked.

"Winn left me this letter."

He eyed me with some skepticism.

"Read it." He took the letter and began to read aloud.

11:34 p.m. Thursday Evening, June 13, 20__:

Dear Souline,

I'm writing you this letter just after I explained your dream to you. I'm writing because I know that my time on this earth is short. I don't know when Christ is coming back; it could be tonight, a month from now, or somewhere in the near future, but I am certain that He will return.

If you are reading this, then just as the angel said, you are not going to be part of Christ's initial return. Although, I so hoped that you would find Christ before He gathered His children this time, but I guess it wasn't meant to be. I know that you didn't believe me when I told you about the angel, but I know that in time you will. I'm not sure what I can say to convince you that I really did talk to him. I tried to tell you what was going to happen, but I know that you needed time to sort things out, especially those things concerning Mom.

I also realize that trying to convince you that I was actually communicating with an angel could be a little unsettling to say the least.

If you're wondering what happened to us, I want you to turn to I Thessalonians 4:16-17, it will explain what I tried to help you to understand. Please read this with an open heart, and an open mind. It might help to put some of your fears to rest. In the time ahead, there are going to be great troubles on the earth. So, I'm leaving you my Bible. Keep it close, it will be the most powerful weapon that you will possess, other than prayer, against the dark powers that are about to come into the world. Know that I'll always love you, and whatever you do, know that you're not alone. Trust in Christ Jesus and know that God loves you, and he will always be with you even until the end.

I love you,

Winn

Oh, P.S.

I know something that might convince you that I was really talking to an angel. The night when I told you about your dream, he told me that just before I leave, you and I would be standing somewhere near each other talking. And you are going to ask me what I meant when I said that, 'In the end you would endure and conquer.'

Your answer is in Matthew 24:13. It says, "But he that shall endure unto the end, the same shall be saved." But I also want you to keep Paul's words before you, Ephesians 6:12-17 says, 'For we wrestle not against flesh and blood, but against principalities, against powers, against the rulers of the darkness of this world, against spiritual wickedness in high places.'

I want you to remember this and take great care when the new world leader, Hadrian Maxmillian, starts to take center stage in the global community, which will be soon. Remember that he was murdered and now he's up walking around! He is extremely dangerous, Souline. His very name means, Great Darkness, and soon, you will understand why. Please read Daniel chapters seven through eleven. No matter what you do, do not take his mark. It will be to your spiritual detriment. Pray that God will keep you strong and watchful and that He will give you wisdom so that you will make it through the dark times that are about to come on the earth. Remember, I love you and Gray. Stay strong, fight with all of your might and always keep God before you.

Your loving sister,

Winn

Gray looked up from the letter, slightly perplexed by the content, but offered no explanation.

I took the letter from his hand and scanned it once more before I folded it, put it in the envelope, and placed it back in the Bible.

"Yesterday, when I was talking to her, I asked her that exact question, verbatim, and just as she was about to answer me, she disappeared." I fought the tiny catch in my voice.

"Honey," he was just about to disagree with me.

"Gray, even you would be hard pressed to answer just how she could have possibly known that I was going to ask her that question before it ever happened." He looked at me and had to admit that he did not have a ready answer for the content of the letter.

"Ordinarily, I would be among the first to wave this away," I continued, "but this is not an ordinary day, is it? My family and a host of others are gone, and I would rather believe this," I patted the Bible that lay on the bed, than a bunch of politicians and news anchormen, spouting a lot of nonsensical spin and speculation about things that they know nothing about. I know my sister, and I know my grandmother and as difficult as it is for me to grasp what happened, I know that neither of them would ever lie to me, or you for that matter. I sighed and looked at the Bible again and said wistfully, "She's one of the one's who won't sleep."

He looked curiously at me and said, "That's an odd turn of phrase."

"But, isn't it true? I think that's how someone said it in the Bible. Something about, "We will not all sleep, but we shall be changed, in a moment, in the twinkling of an eye". It has to do with the Rapture.

He stared at me with mild surprise on his face, and asked, "Is that what you believe?"

A wisp of a smile tinged with regret touched my lips, as I wiped a tear from my face that had rolled down my cheek. "For most of my life, I've been fighting a dream, something in my life that I had not understood. My family had tried their best to make me see that there was something better, something greater than myself to believe in, but I ignored them because of a bitterness that I had been carrying in my heart since my mother's death. And now I've got nothing. No mother, no family, no nothing! I sniff mildly, and Grayson handed me a handkerchief from his shirt pocket. "If I'm going to see them again, it's what I must believe," I said with conviction.

"I'm all alone now," I said with a quiet resignation, as the reality of the loss of Winn and Gran began to settle in.

"That's not true," he said, his gaze steady and determined. "You've got me."

I touched his hand and brought it to my cheek. "Yes," I said softly. I've got you." I smiled and kissed him. "I've got you and I love you, Grayson."

"I love you too, Soul," He said, and smiled as he lightly ran a finger across my cheek and kissed me.

"And you know what else, I've got?" I asked.

He shook his head, and quietly asked, "No, what?"

"Faith," I said. "Faith in all that my sister and my grandmother had been trying to tell me about God. And you know what else?"

He smiled and shook his head again.

"I'm not going to let them down, Gray. I'm determined that I'm going to see them again. I promise you I will. I'm going to fight, and I'll do whatever it takes to see my family again.

I know that I've got things to figure out, but I also know that if they are in heaven, I want to see them again. And, if their faith in God took them beyond this place, then I want to find out why, and how."

He did not try to argue with me when he saw the fiery determination that had settled on my face; a face that he had seen go through a multitude of emotions in such a short period of time. He hugged and kissed me, and stood up and said, "I don't have an easy answer for what's happened, but I do know that whatever the future holds good or bad I want to share it with you."

Before I Wake

There was a sense of warmth that washed over me as I looked in those brown eyes. A great sense of belonging filled my heart. At that moment, I knew that I would always want to be with him. I knew that I would always want to be in his life, and I knew that I wanted him to be in mine.

Let's go, beautiful," he said, as he held his hand out to me.

I smiled and reached for the proffered hand as I walked toward the door. But before I took it, I stopped, turned, and hurried back toward the bed. His brows furrowed slightly, wondering what prompted the action.

I smiled as I walked back toward him.

"I forgot my Bible," I said, holding the most precious gift my sister had given me.

I grabbed his hand linking my fingers in his. I noticed that I could not tell where his began or where my ended. Like a puzzle, they seemed to fit. There was a warm sensation of belonging that washed over me.

"I love you, Gray," I said and looked up at him.

"I love you too Souline," he smiled and kissed me again.

As we walked out of the room, the mist that I had been fighting all morning seemed to finally lift from my mind. The headache that I had started to ease and the heavy fog began to dissipate. I heard the rude interruption of that hateful alarm clock gnawing through my subconscious.

"Souline," I heard my name and a gentle knock. "Souline honey," I heard the familiar voice calling my name and I eased up on one elbow in bed and yawned rubbing the sleep from my eyes.

"What a night," I mumbled through another yawn. "That was the strangest dream." I heard another gentle knock at the door that managed to penetrate through my muzzy brain. There was a tiny squeak from the hinge on my bedroom door.

"Grayson just called to say that he was on his way to pick you up to take you to breakfast." The soft voice said.

"Winn, is that you?" I asked with a yawn, slightly bewildered.

"Of course it is who else would it be silly?" She said, with a pert giggle. "It's time to wake up."